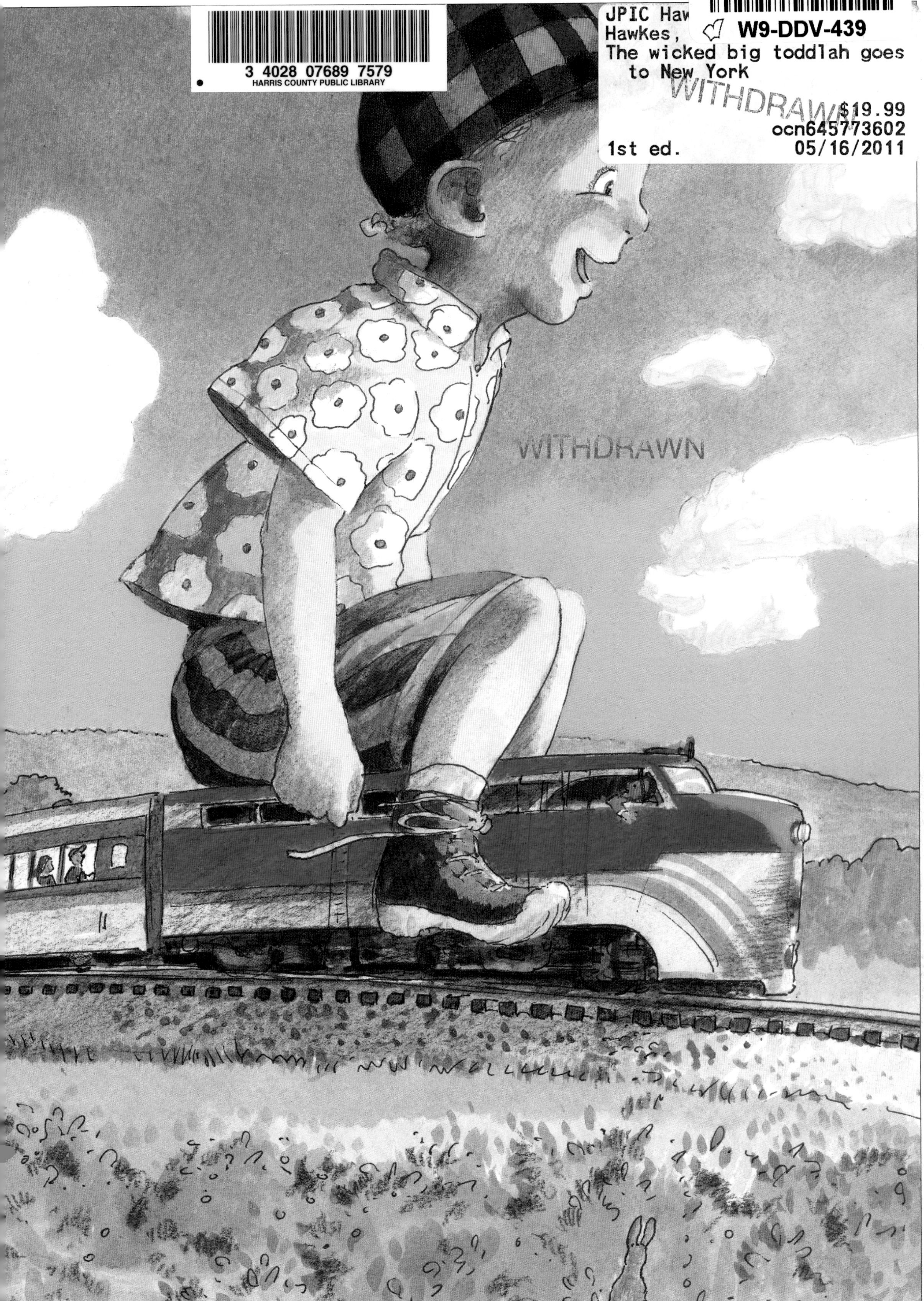

THIS IS A BORZOI BOOK PUBLISHED BY ALFRED A. KNOPF

Visit us on the Web! www.randomhouse.com/kids

Educators and librarians, for a variety of teaching tools, visit us at
www.randomhouse.com/teachers

Library of Congress Cataloging-in-Publication Data
Hawkes, Kevin.
The wicked big toddlah goes to New York / Kevin Hawkes. — 1st ed.
p. cm.
Summary: A Maine couple and their gigantic toddler take a trip to New York City, where despite his size, the "wicked big toddlah" becomes lost.
ISBN 978-0-375-86188-8 (trade) — ISBN 978-0-375-96189-2 (lib. bdg.)
[1. Toddlers—Fiction. 2. Size—Fiction. 3. Lost children—Fiction. 4. New York (N.Y.)—Fiction.] I. Title. II. Title: Wicked big toddlah goes to New York.
PZ7.H31324Wk 2010
[E]—dc22
2009048258

The text of this book is set in 17-point Goudy.
The illustrations in this book were created using India ink, charcoal, and acrylic.

MANUFACTURED IN CHINA

April 2011

10 9 8 7 6 5 4 3 2 1

First Edition

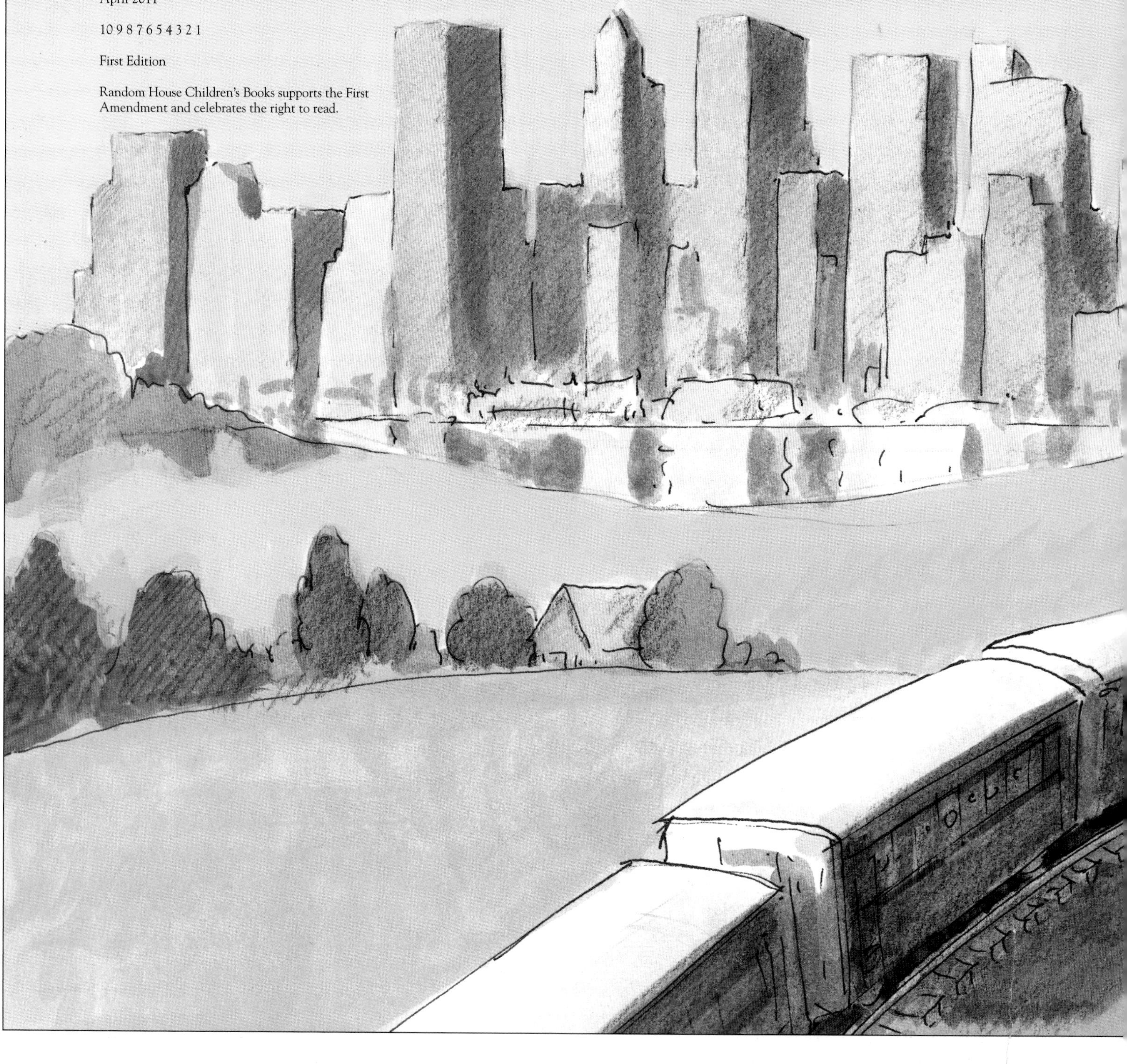

THE WICKED BIG TODDLAH GOES TO NEW YORK

KEVIN HAWKES

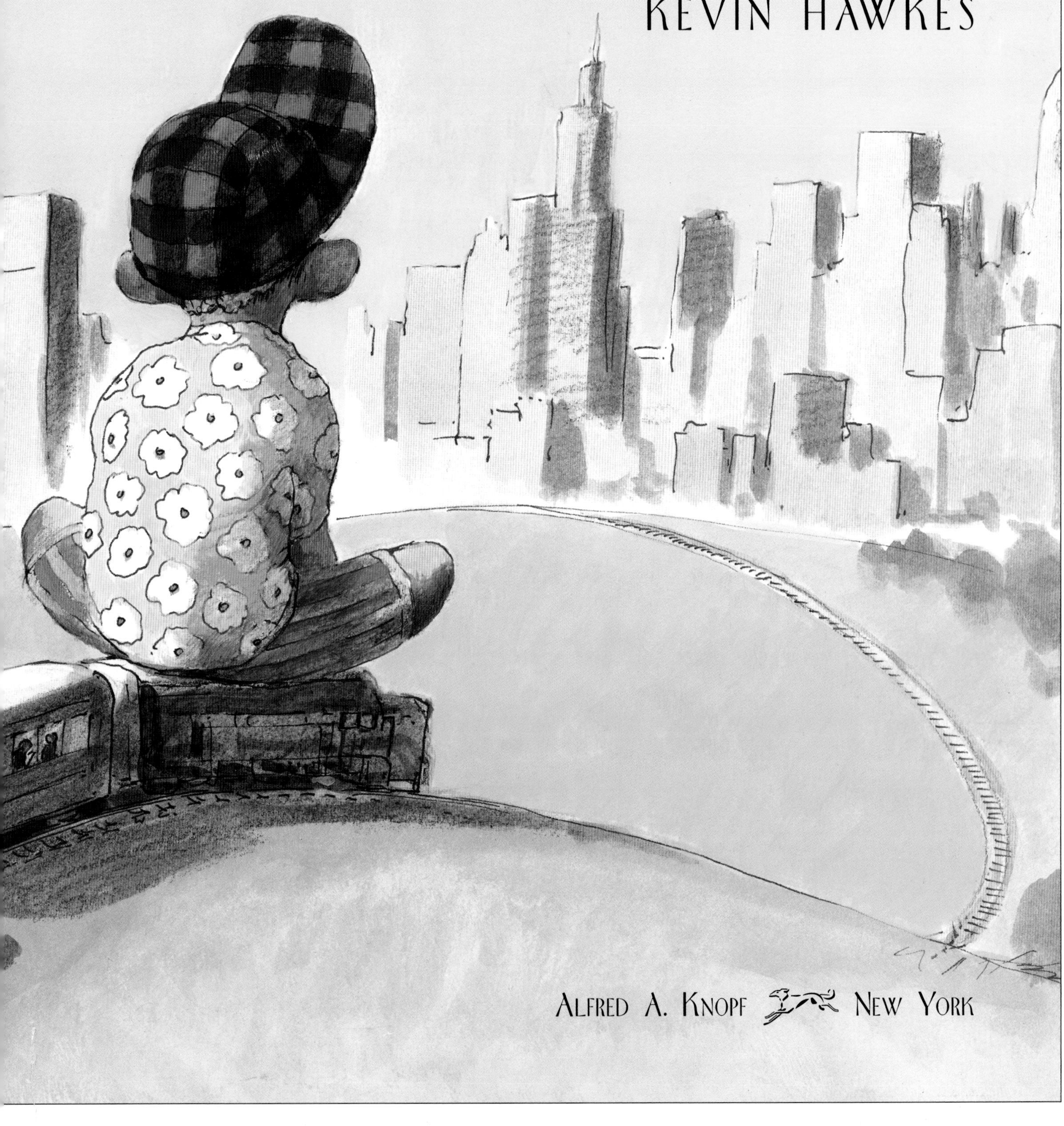

ALFRED A. KNOPF NEW YORK

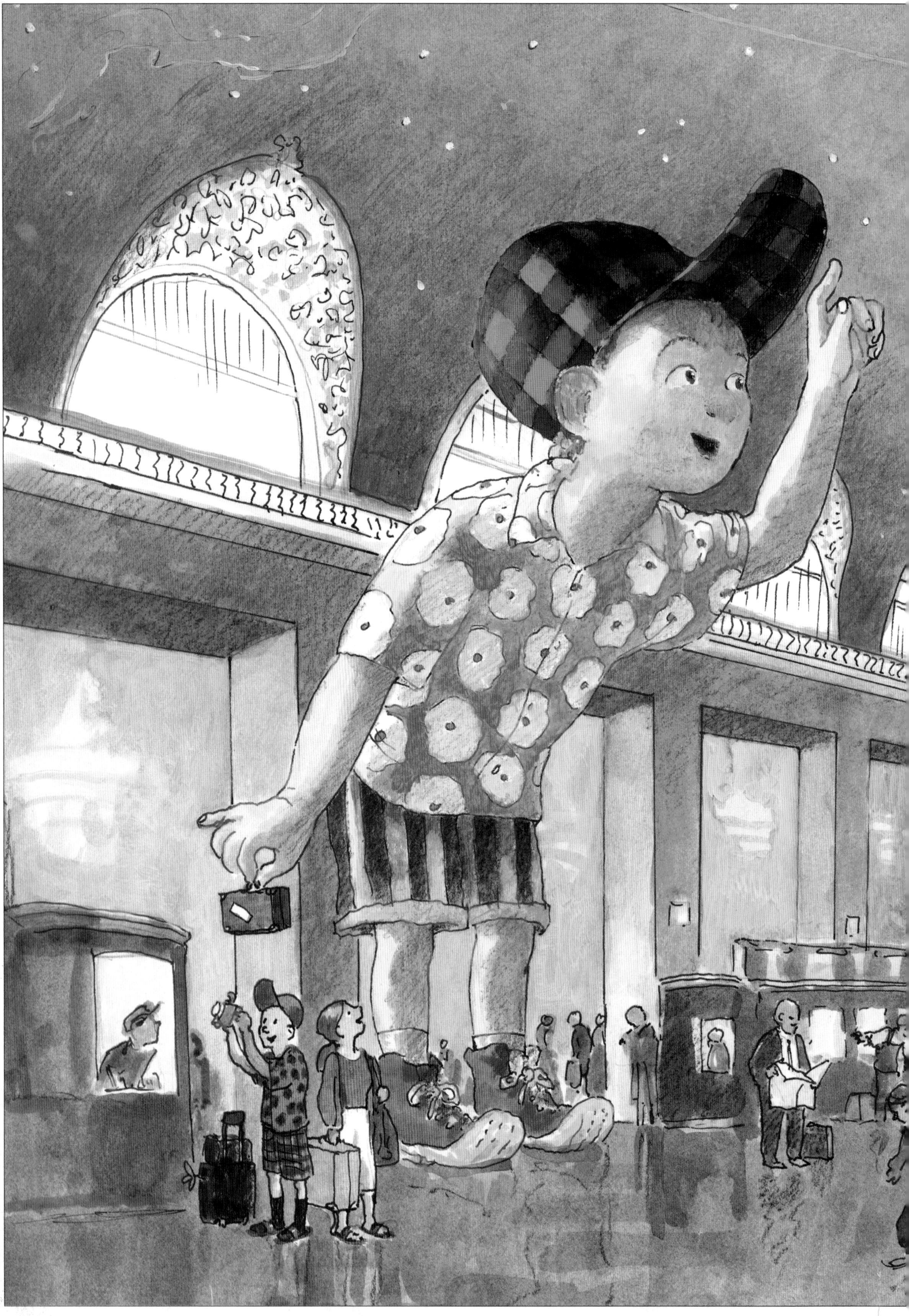

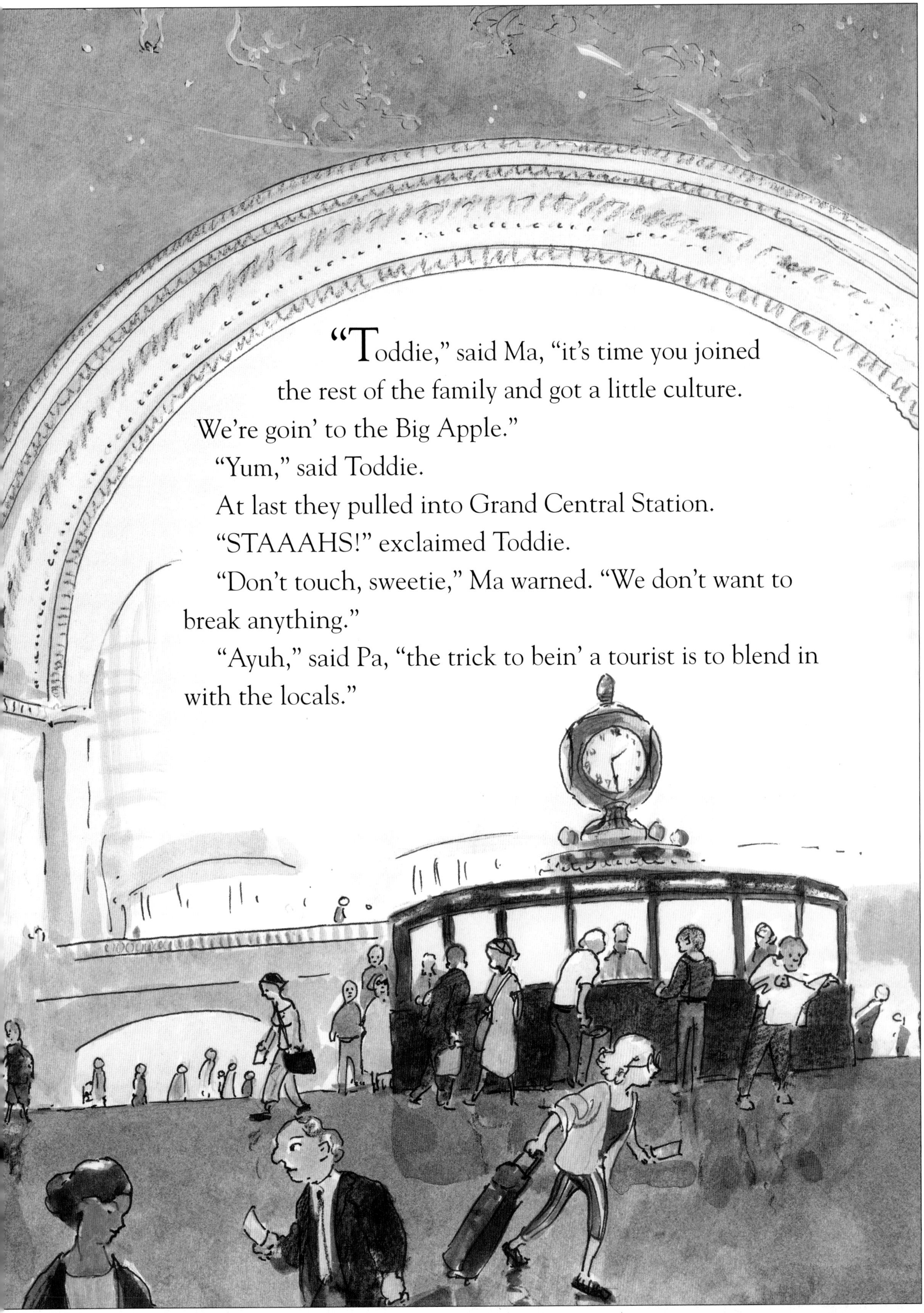

"Toddie," said Ma, "it's time you joined the rest of the family and got a little culture. We're goin' to the Big Apple."

"Yum," said Toddie.

At last they pulled into Grand Central Station.

"STAAAHS!" exclaimed Toddie.

"Don't touch, sweetie," Ma warned. "We don't want to break anything."

"Ayuh," said Pa, "the trick to bein' a tourist is to blend in with the locals."

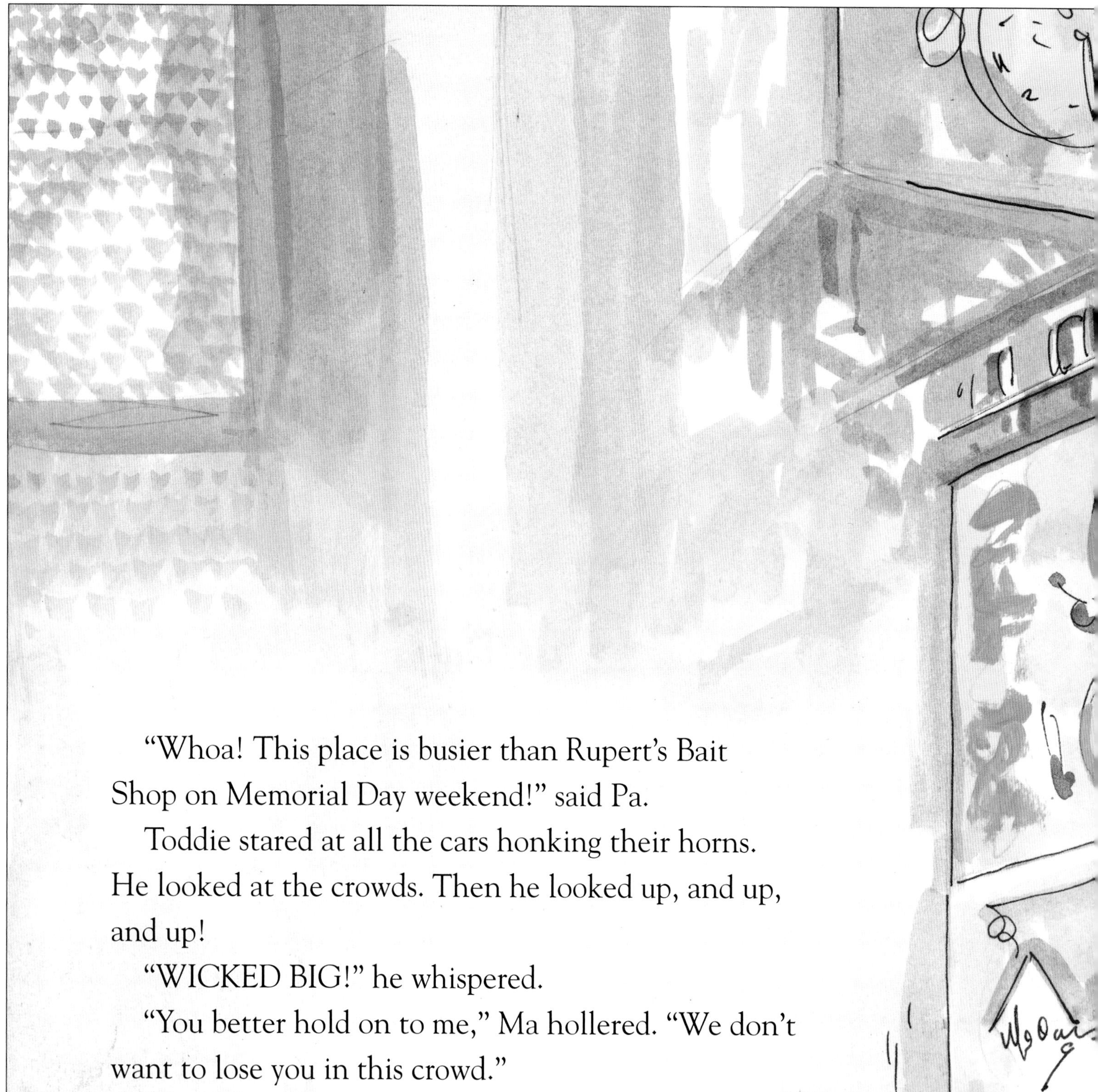

"Whoa! This place is busier than Rupert's Bait Shop on Memorial Day weekend!" said Pa.

Toddie stared at all the cars honking their horns. He looked at the crowds. Then he looked up, and up, and up!

"WICKED BIG!" he whispered.

"You better hold on to me," Ma hollered. "We don't want to lose you in this crowd."

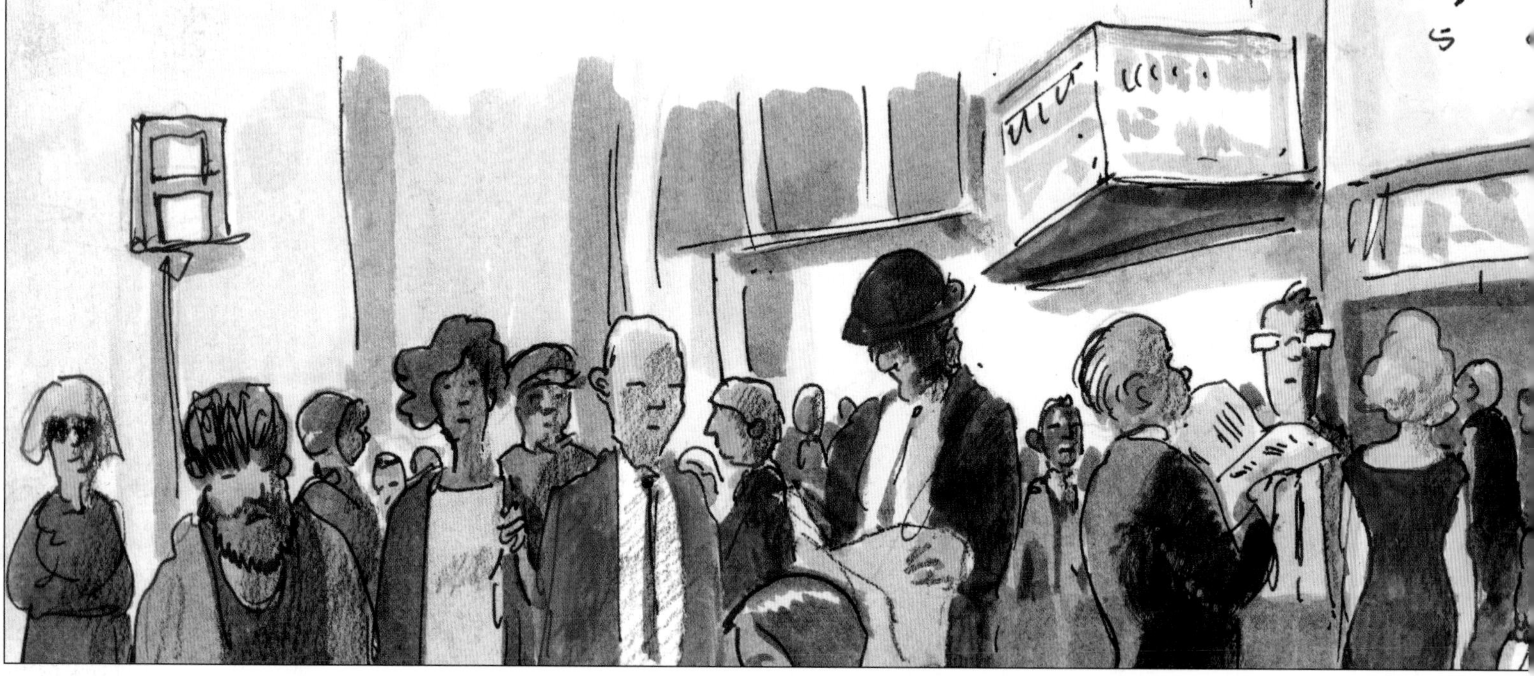

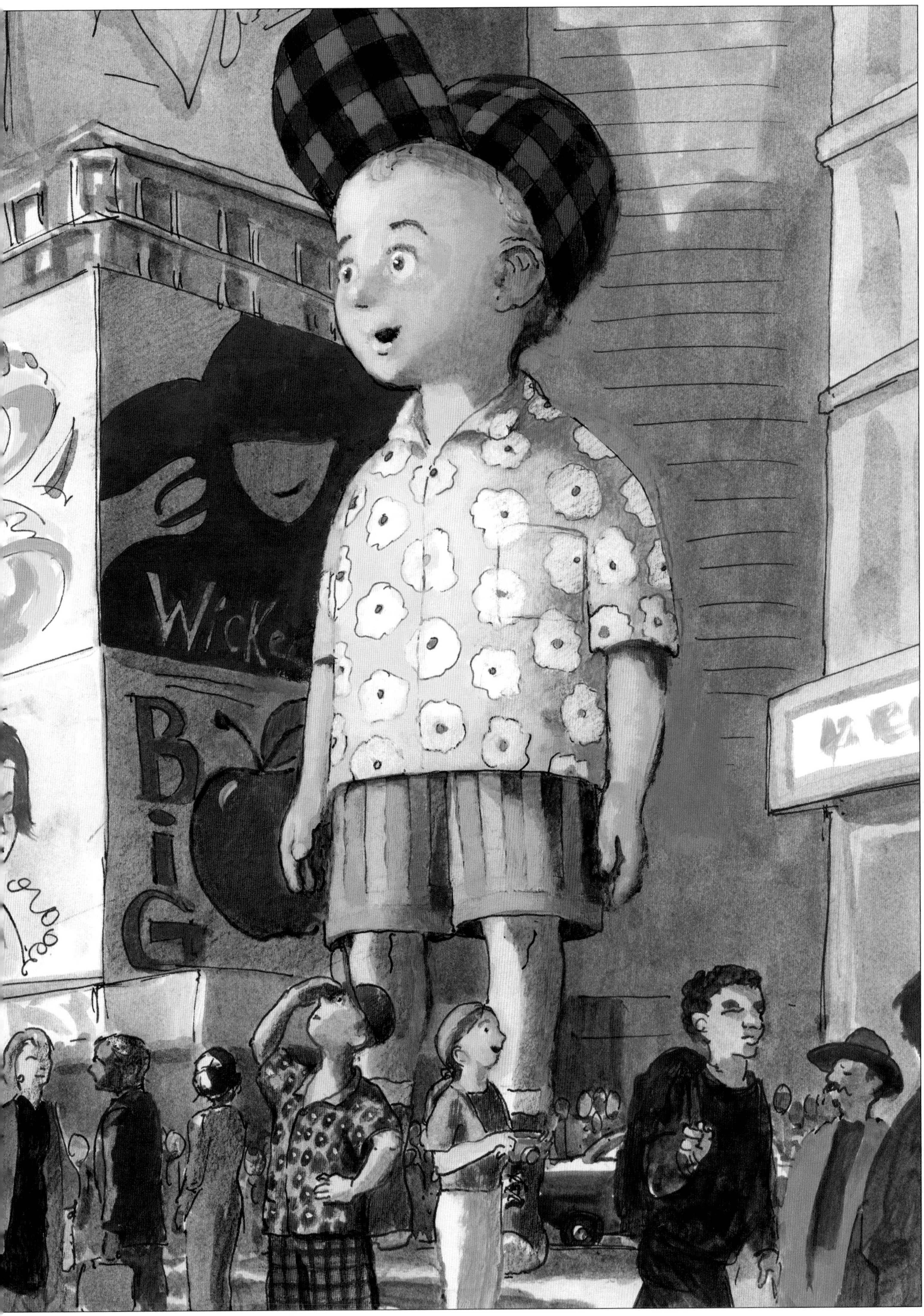
BiG

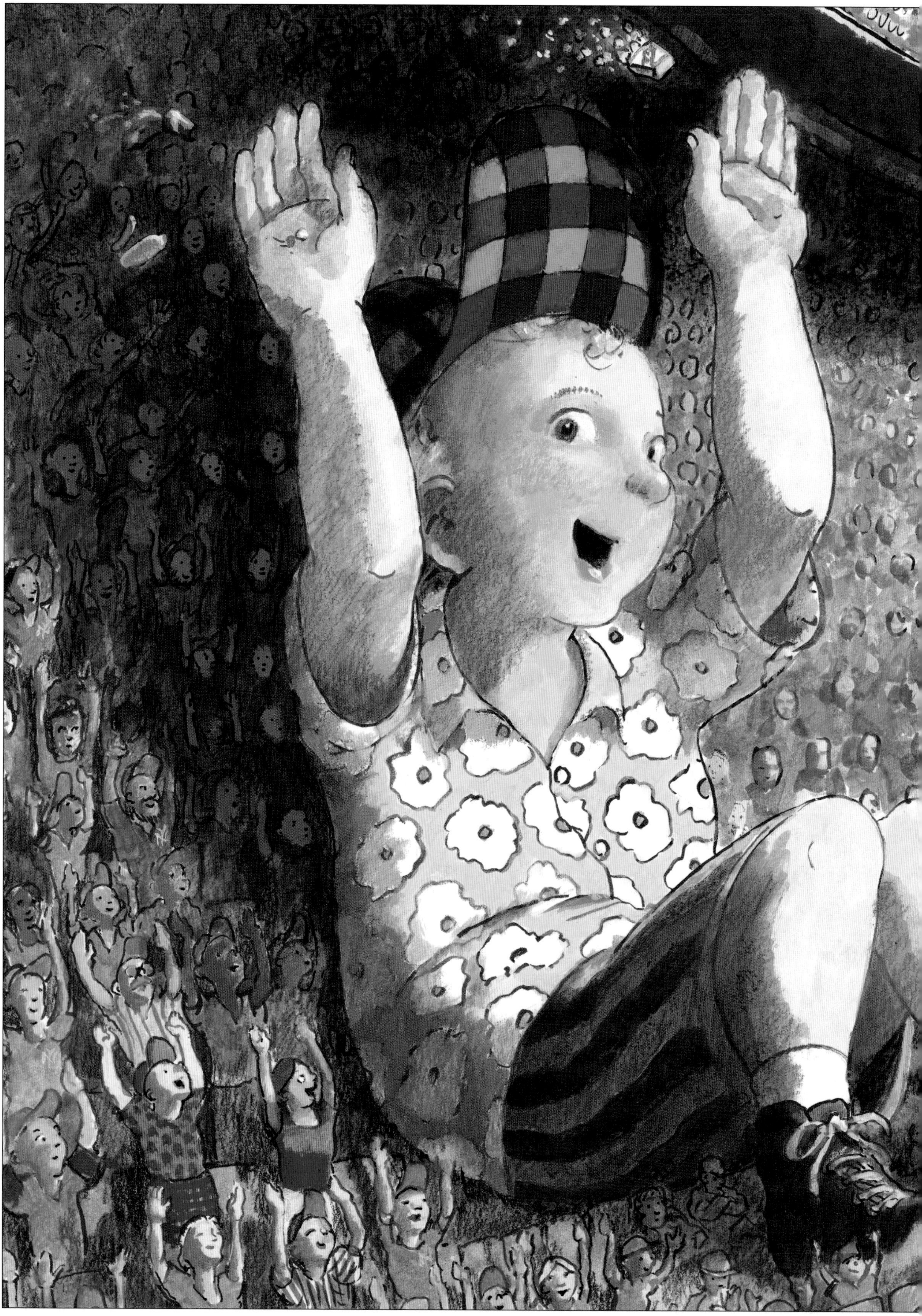

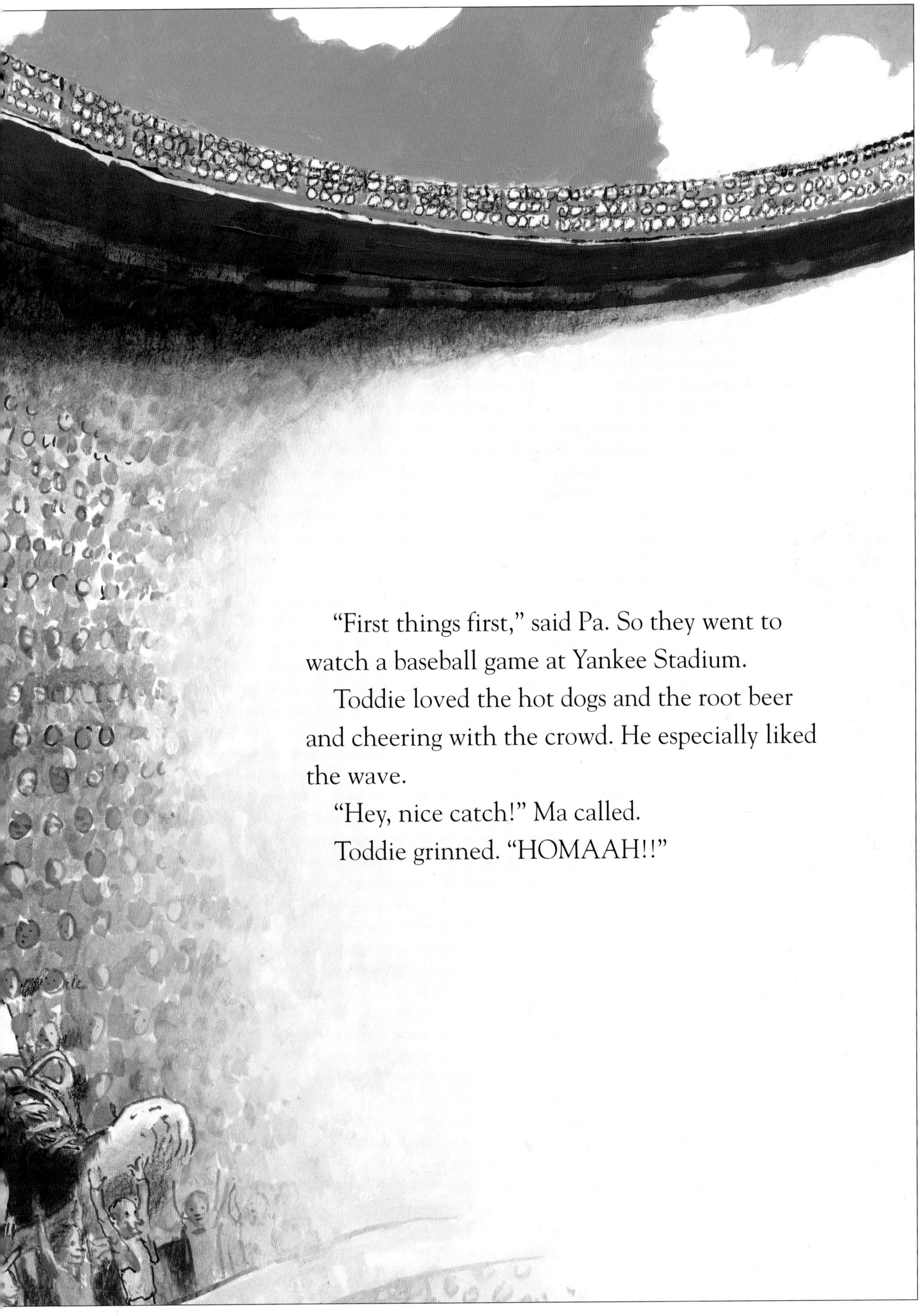

“First things first,” said Pa. So they went to watch a baseball game at Yankee Stadium.

Toddie loved the hot dogs and the root beer and cheering with the crowd. He especially liked the wave.

“Hey, nice catch!” Ma called.

Toddie grinned. “HOMAAH!!”

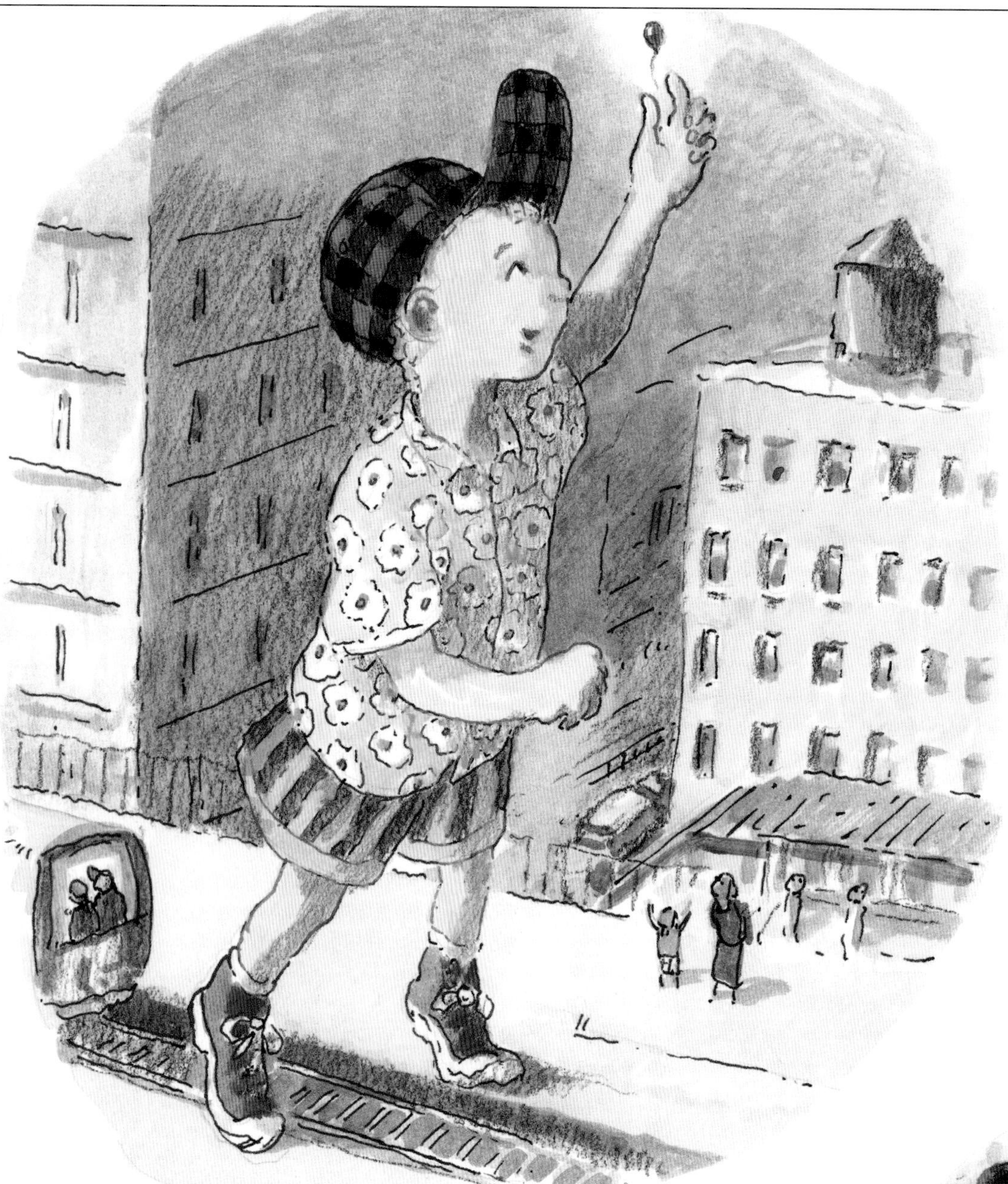

"My feet feel like flapjacks!" Ma said after the game. "Let's take the train."

At one stop, a little girl lost her balloon. As it floated away, Toddie jumped and caught it for her.

But when he turned back, the train was gone!

"Ma? Pa?" he whispered.

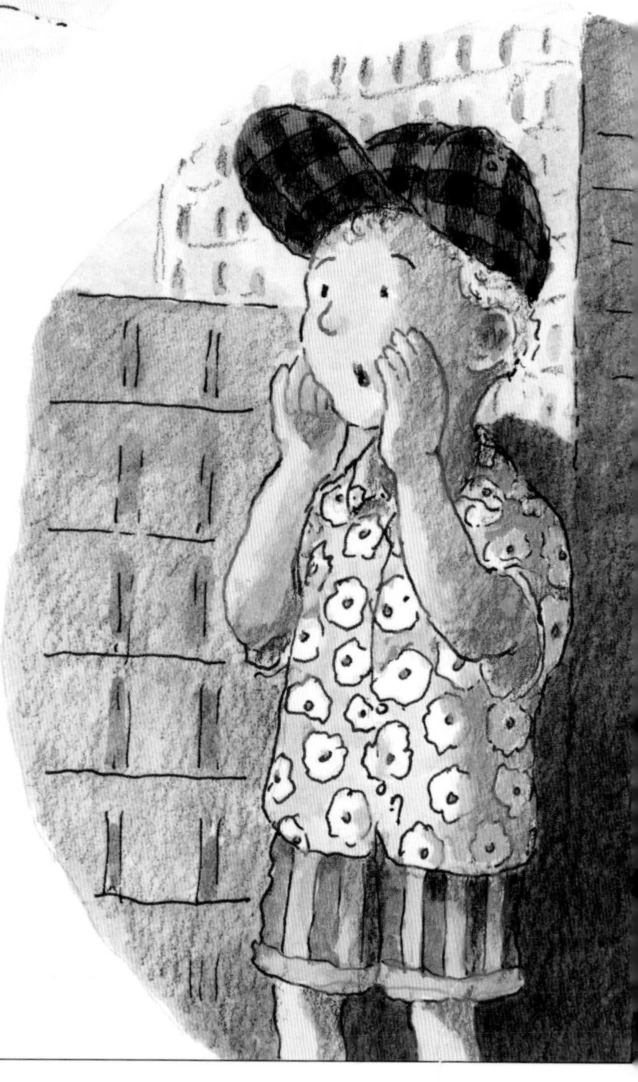

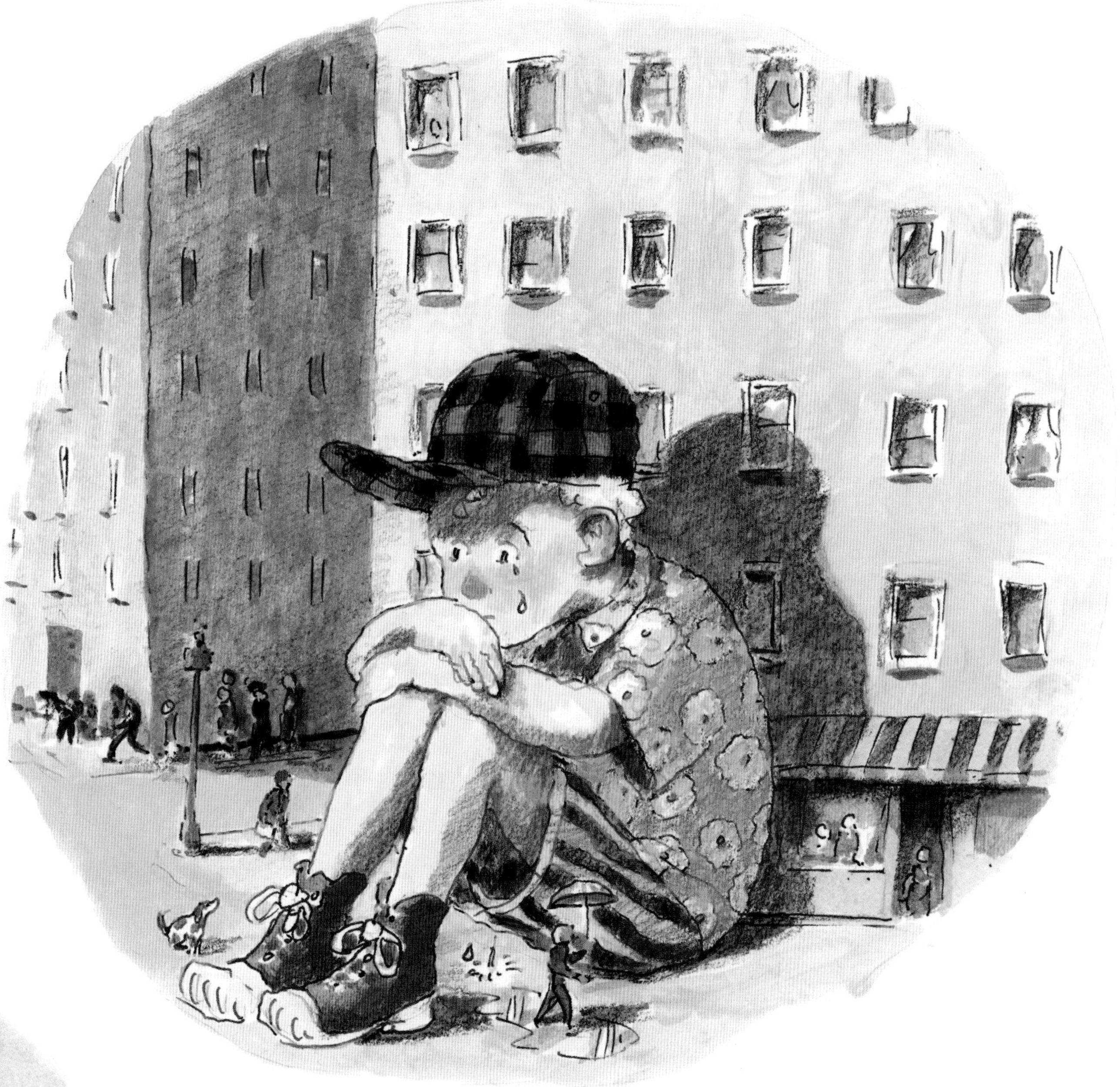

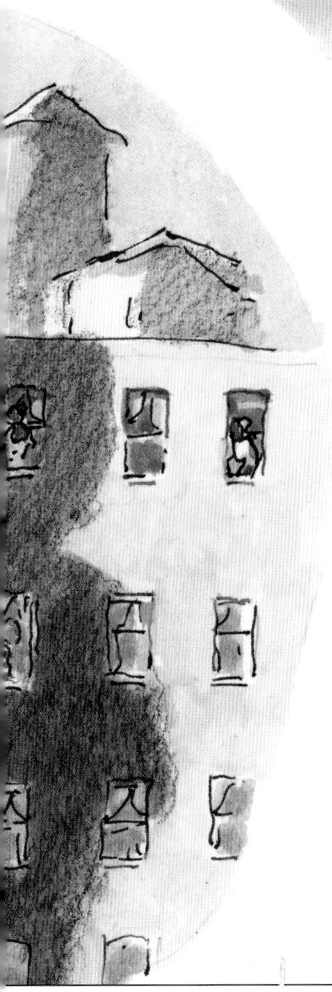

Toddie searched and searched. He was tired and hungry and scared. Giant tears welled out of the corners of his eyes and splashed onto the sidewalk.

Ruff!

Toddie opened his eyes. It was a dog! Toddie gave her a gentle pat. "Lost, too?"

Ruff!

The dog trotted down the sidewalk, and Toddie followed her around a corner. There was a tall statue and a fountain! There were people and trees and dogs and . . .

"TODDLAHS!!" Toddie shouted.

"Hey!" a little boy hollered. "Wanna play?"

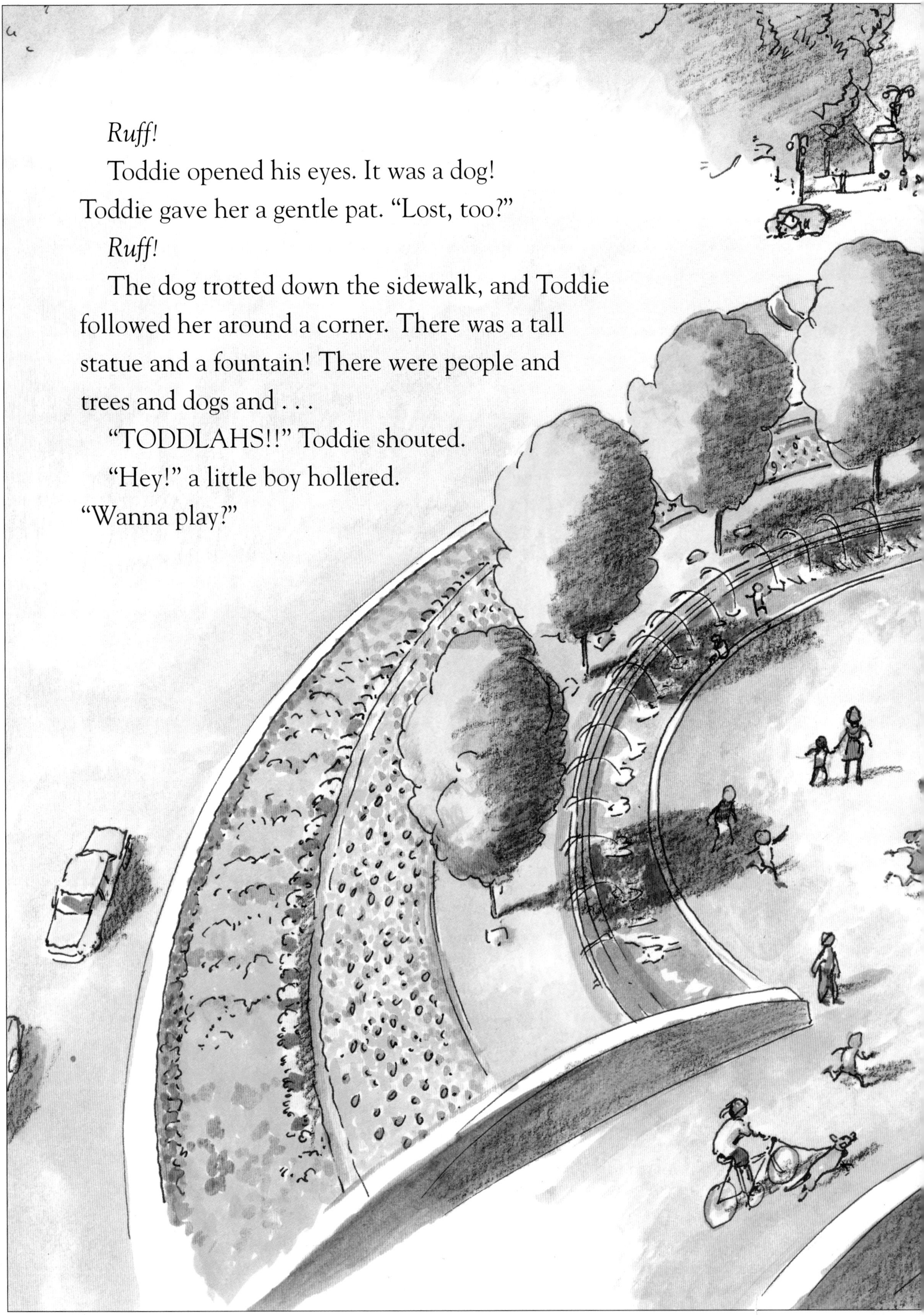

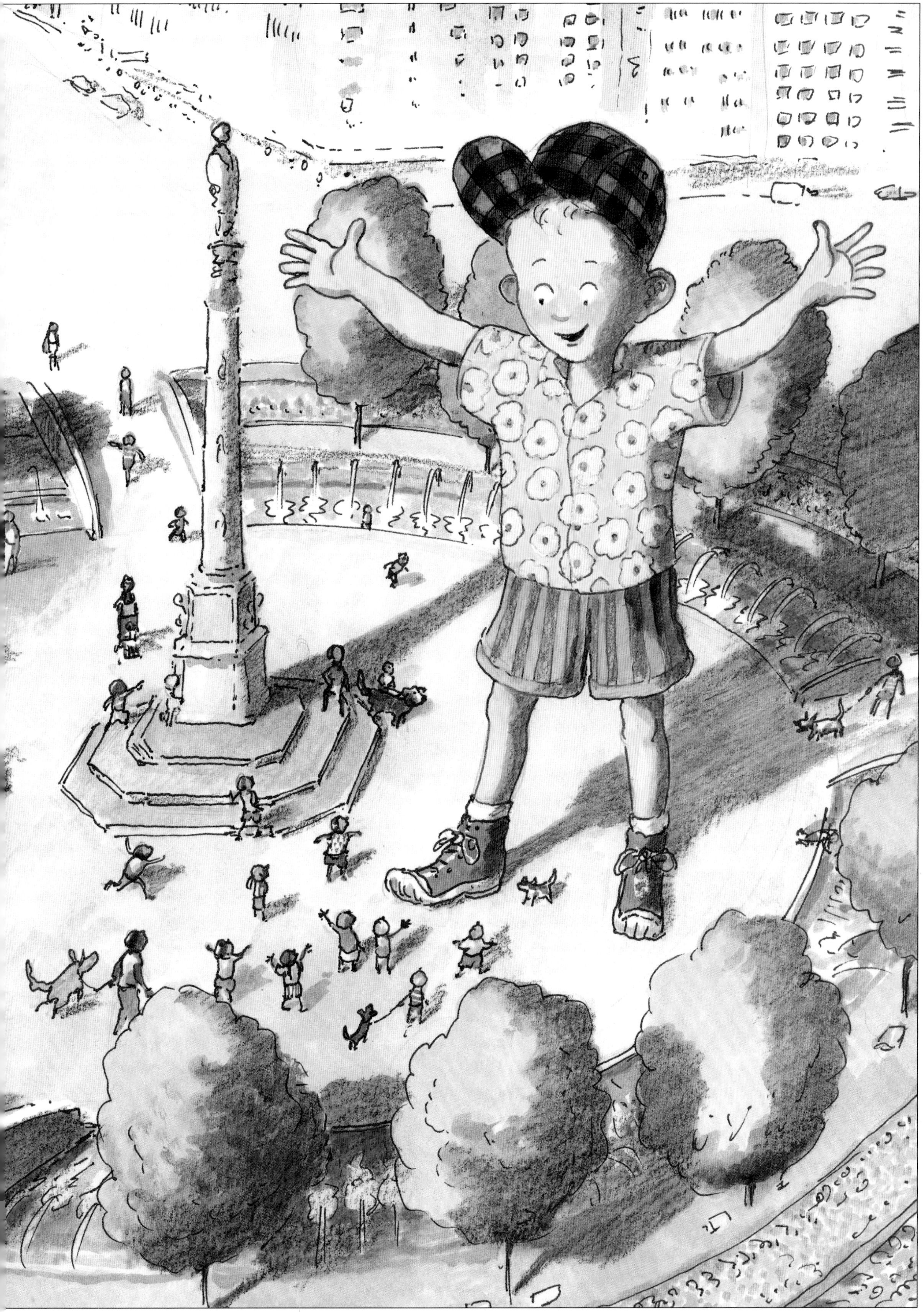

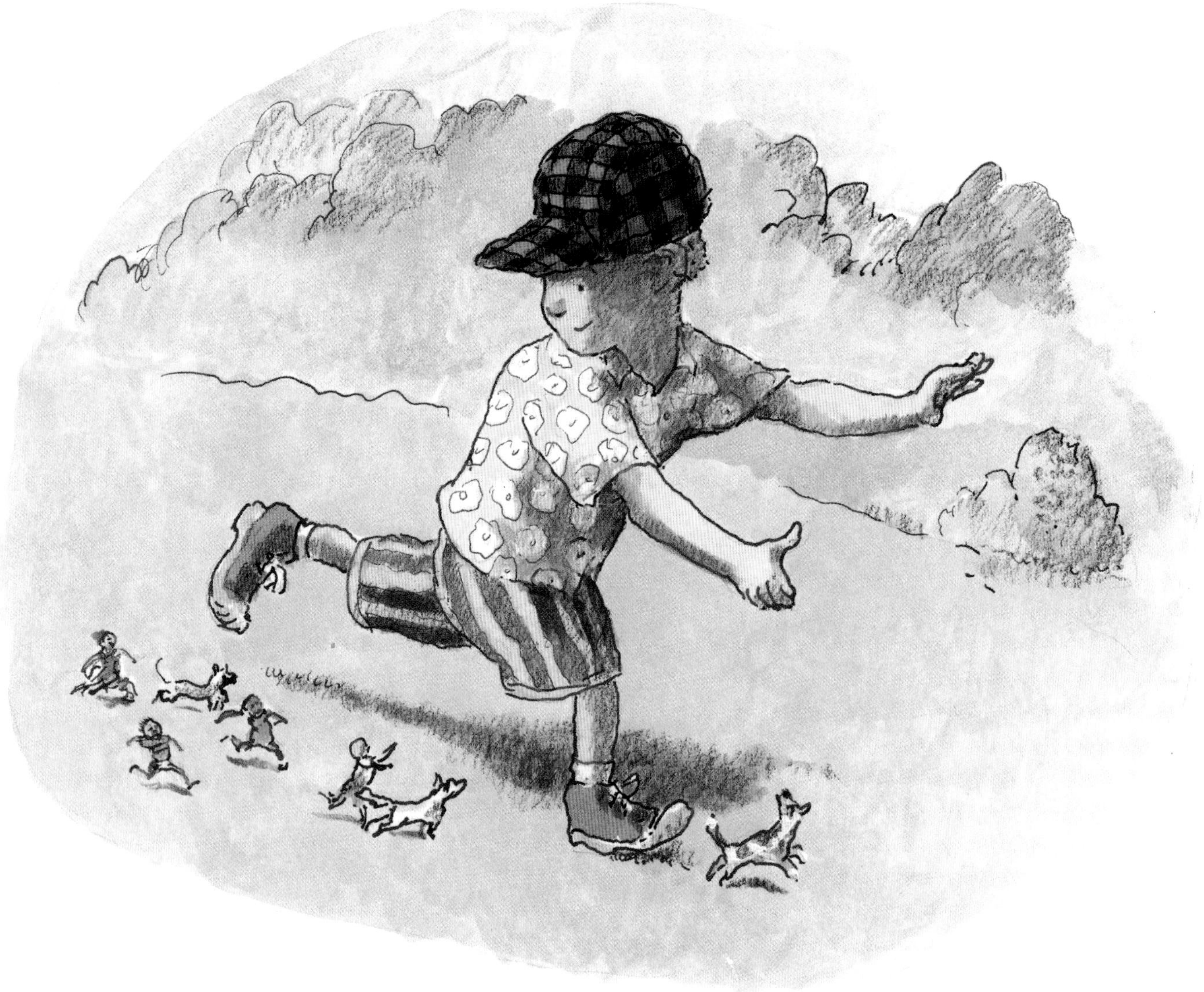

Toddie and his new friends played tag

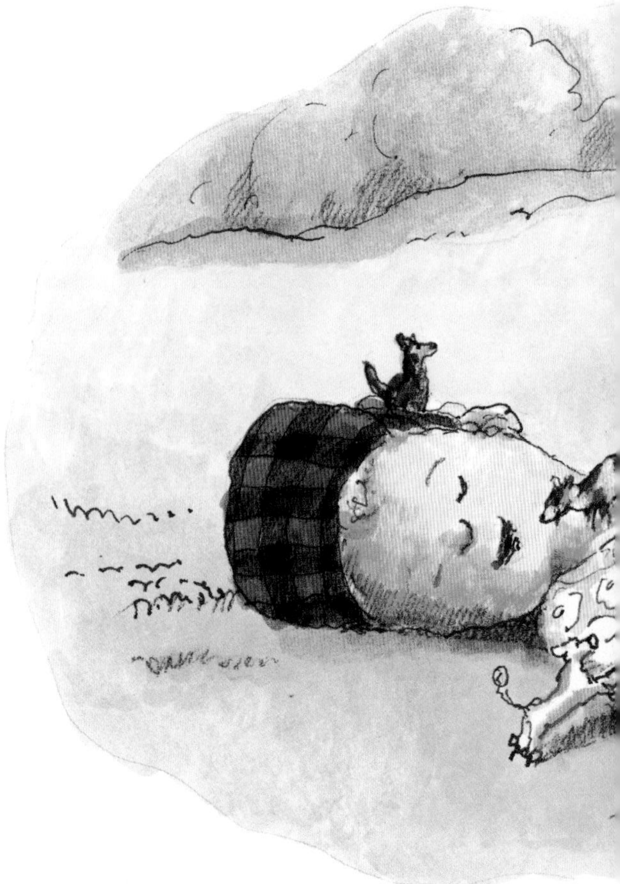

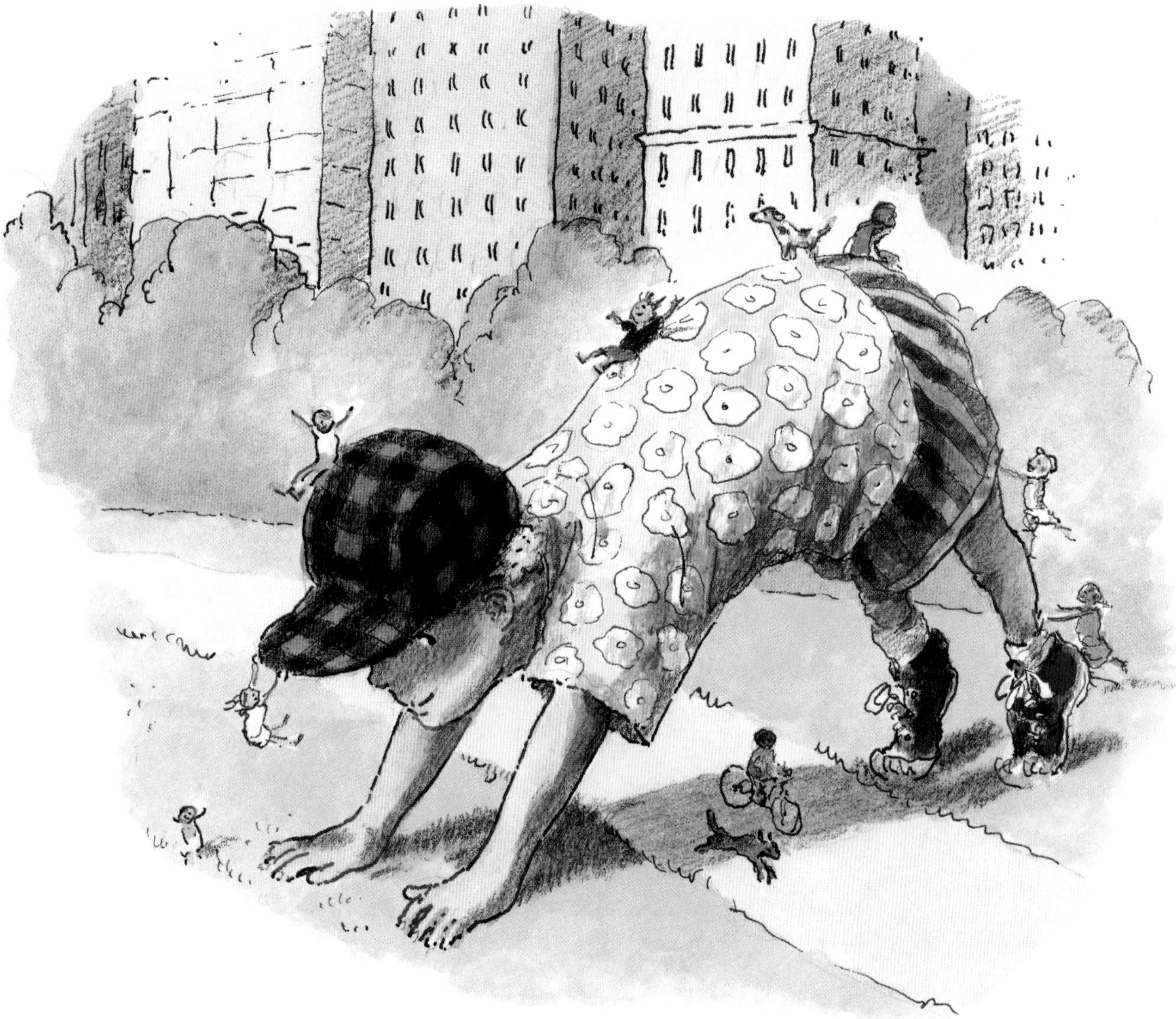

and London Bridge

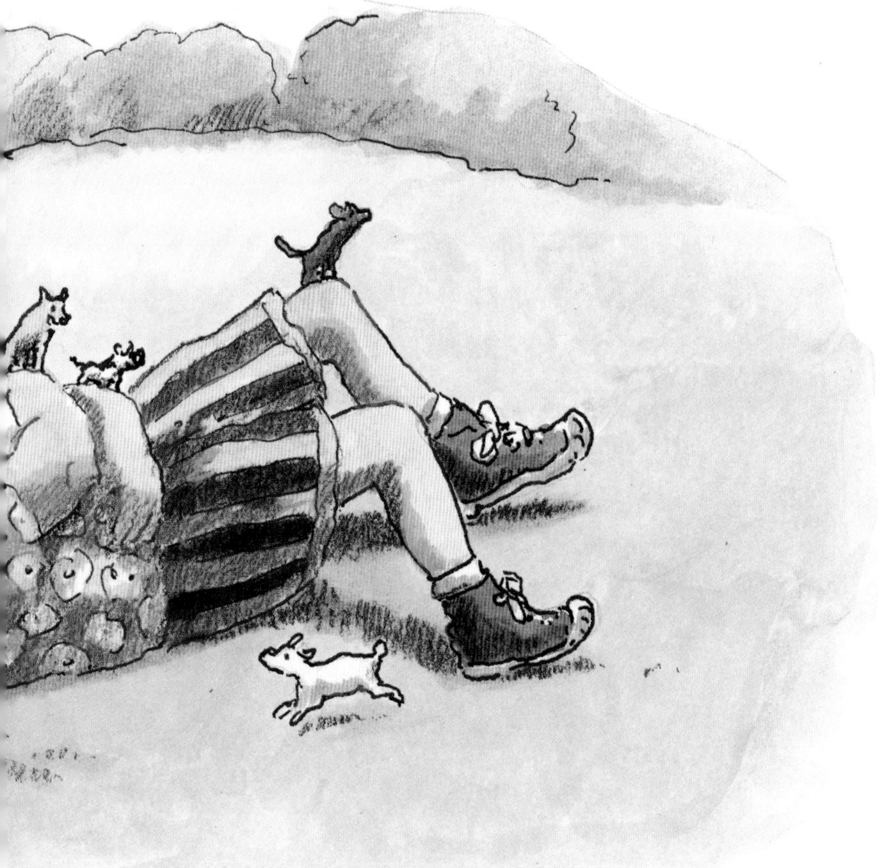

and king of the hill.

They played boats and hide-and-seek. They even had a snack with the pretzel man.

"Here, Bingo." A boy and a girl came running
down the sidewalk. Toddie smiled. His doggie
had found her family at last.

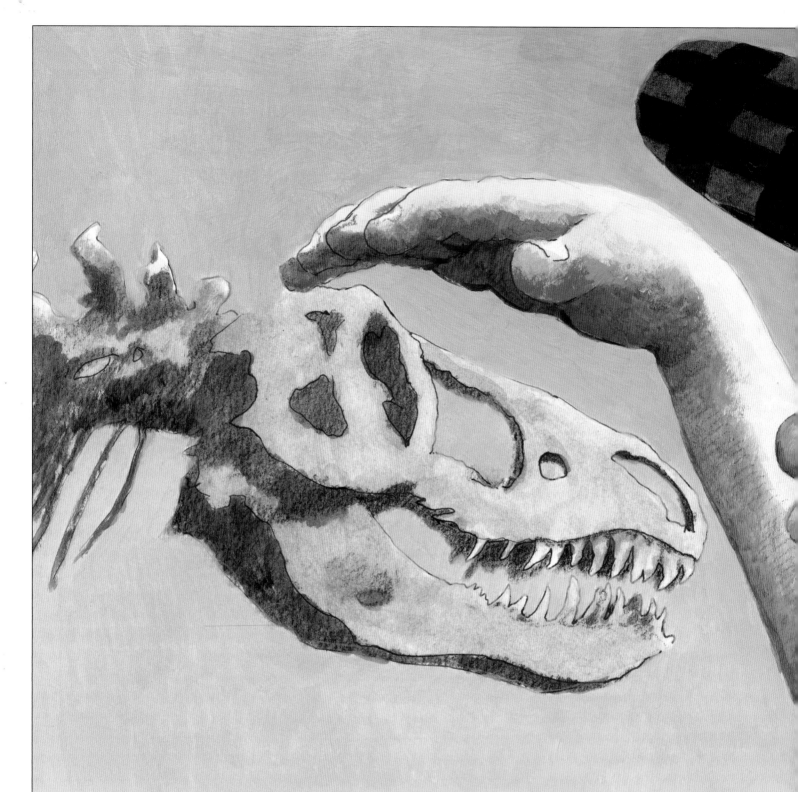

"Would you all like to go to the Museum of
Natural History with us?" the children asked.
"Ayuh," said Toddie.
They saw elephants and blue whales and
even a Tyrannosaurus rex!
"Nice doggie!" breathed Toddie.

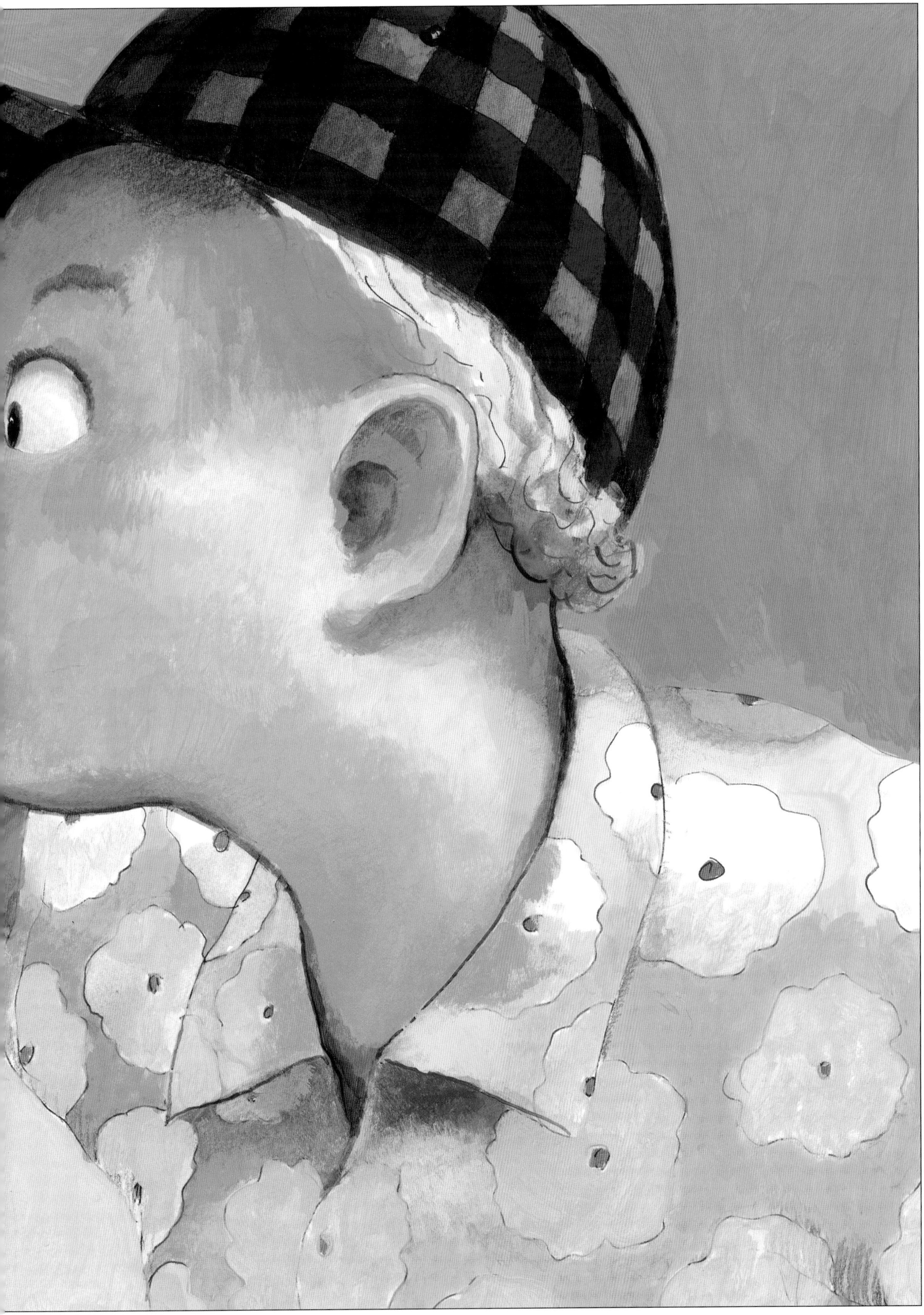

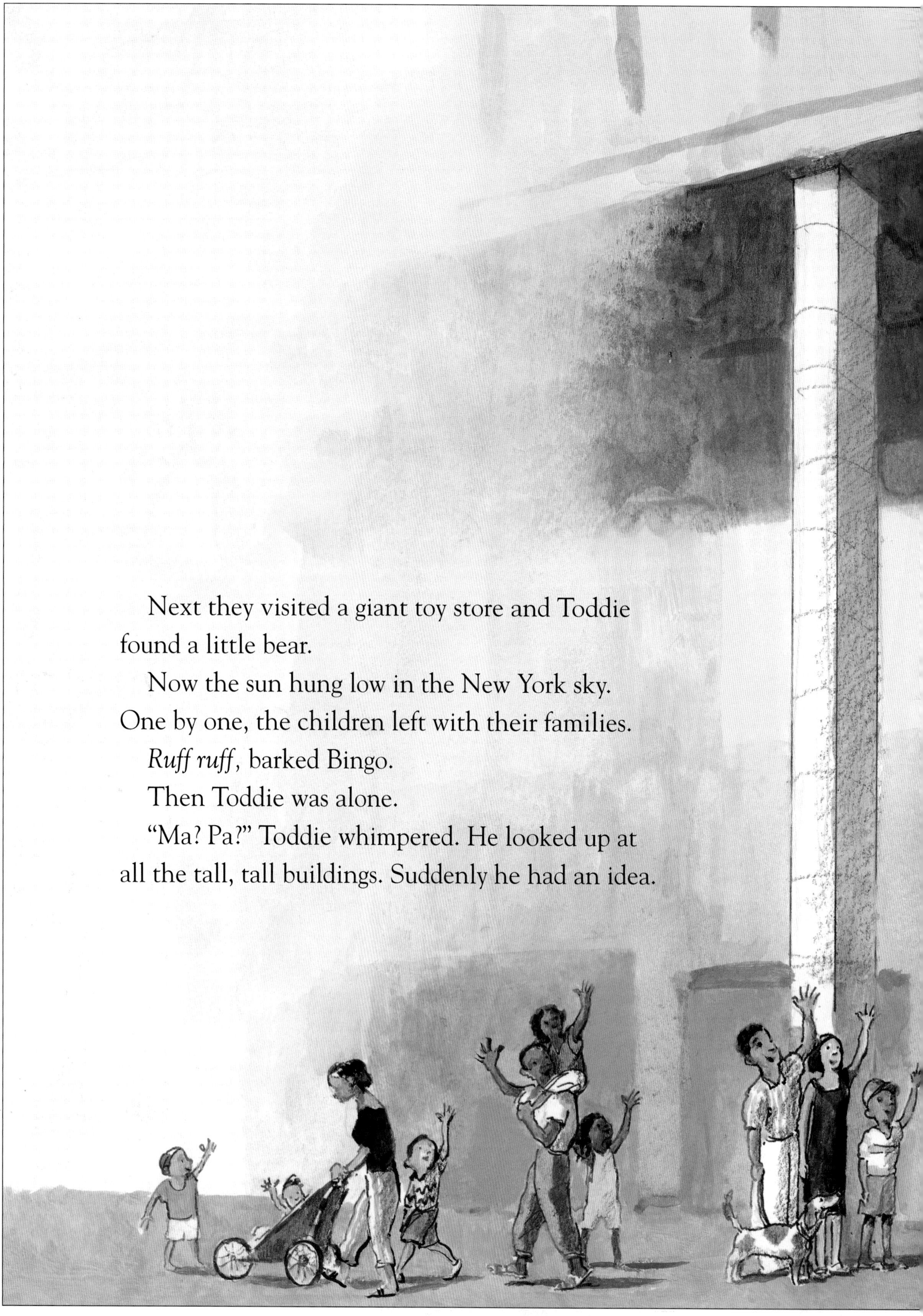

Next they visited a giant toy store and Toddie found a little bear.

Now the sun hung low in the New York sky. One by one, the children left with their families.

Ruff ruff, barked Bingo.

Then Toddie was alone.

"Ma? Pa?" Toddie whimpered. He looked up at all the tall, tall buildings. Suddenly he had an idea.

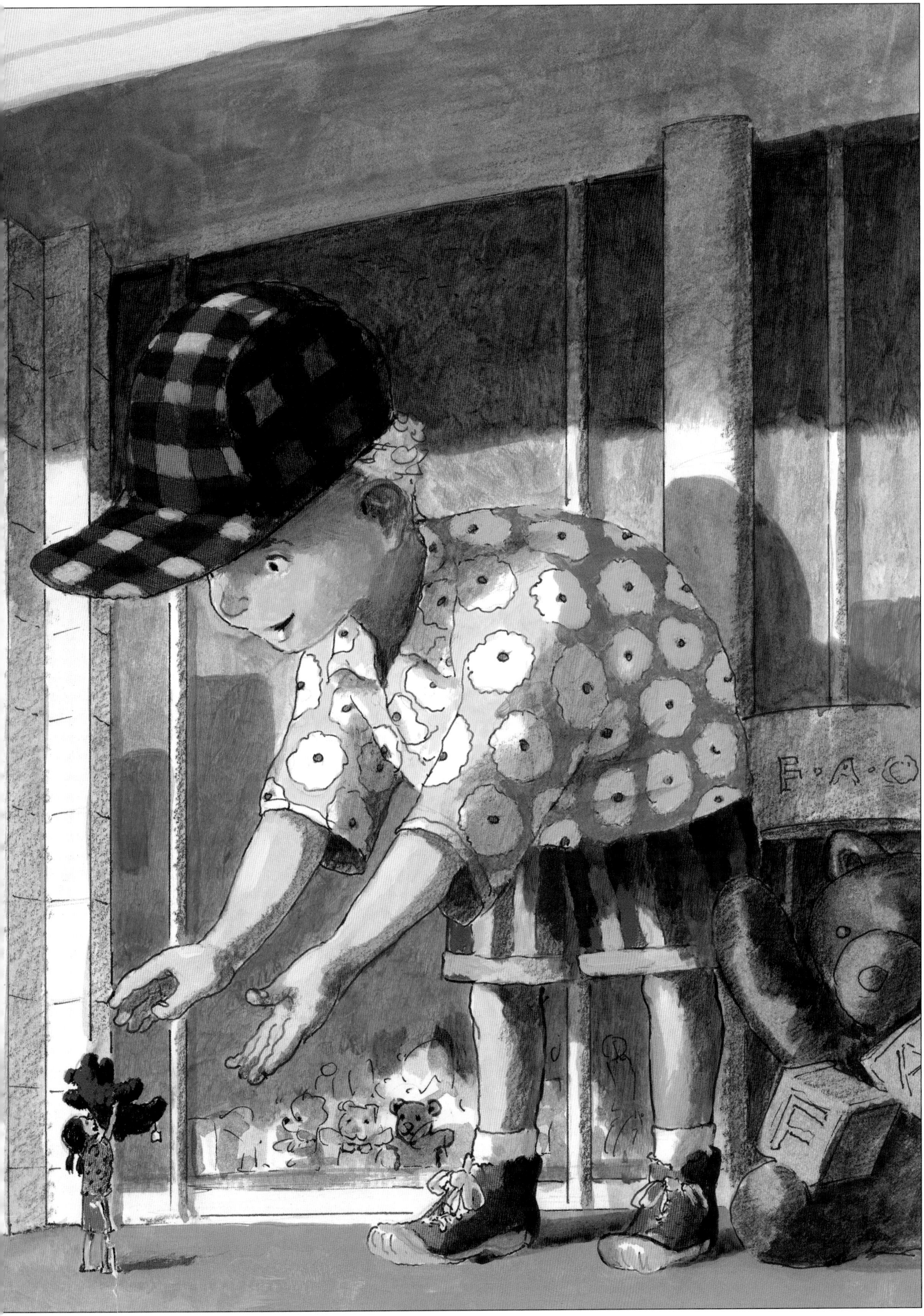
F·A·O

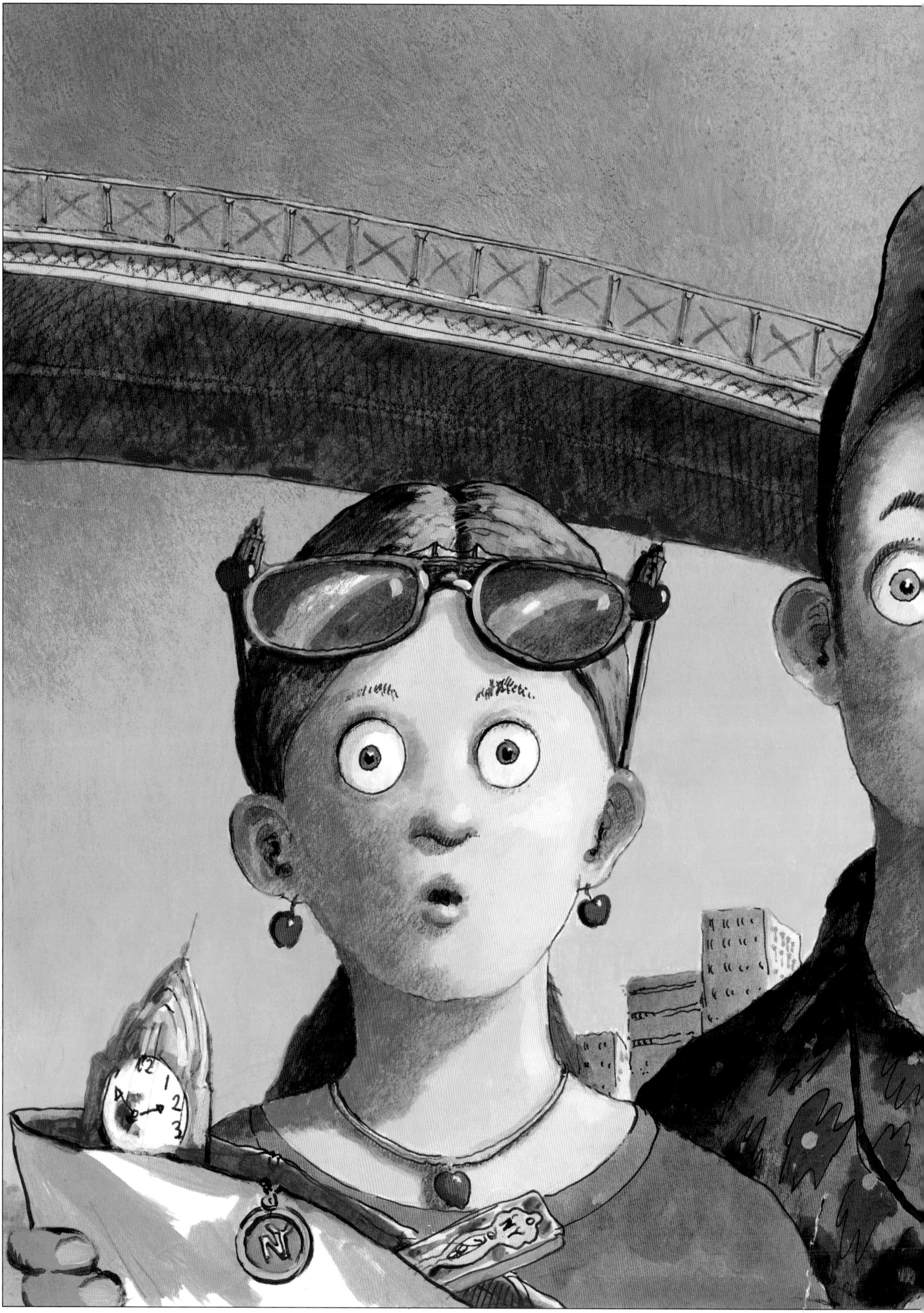

Meanwhile, Ma and Pa were busy snapping pictures.

"Let's get a photo of you and Toddie at the Brooklyn Bridge," suggested Pa.

"Toddie!" said Ma. "I thought *you* had him."

"I thought *you* had him," said Pa.

"Leapin' lobstahs!! Where's Toddie!?!?!?"

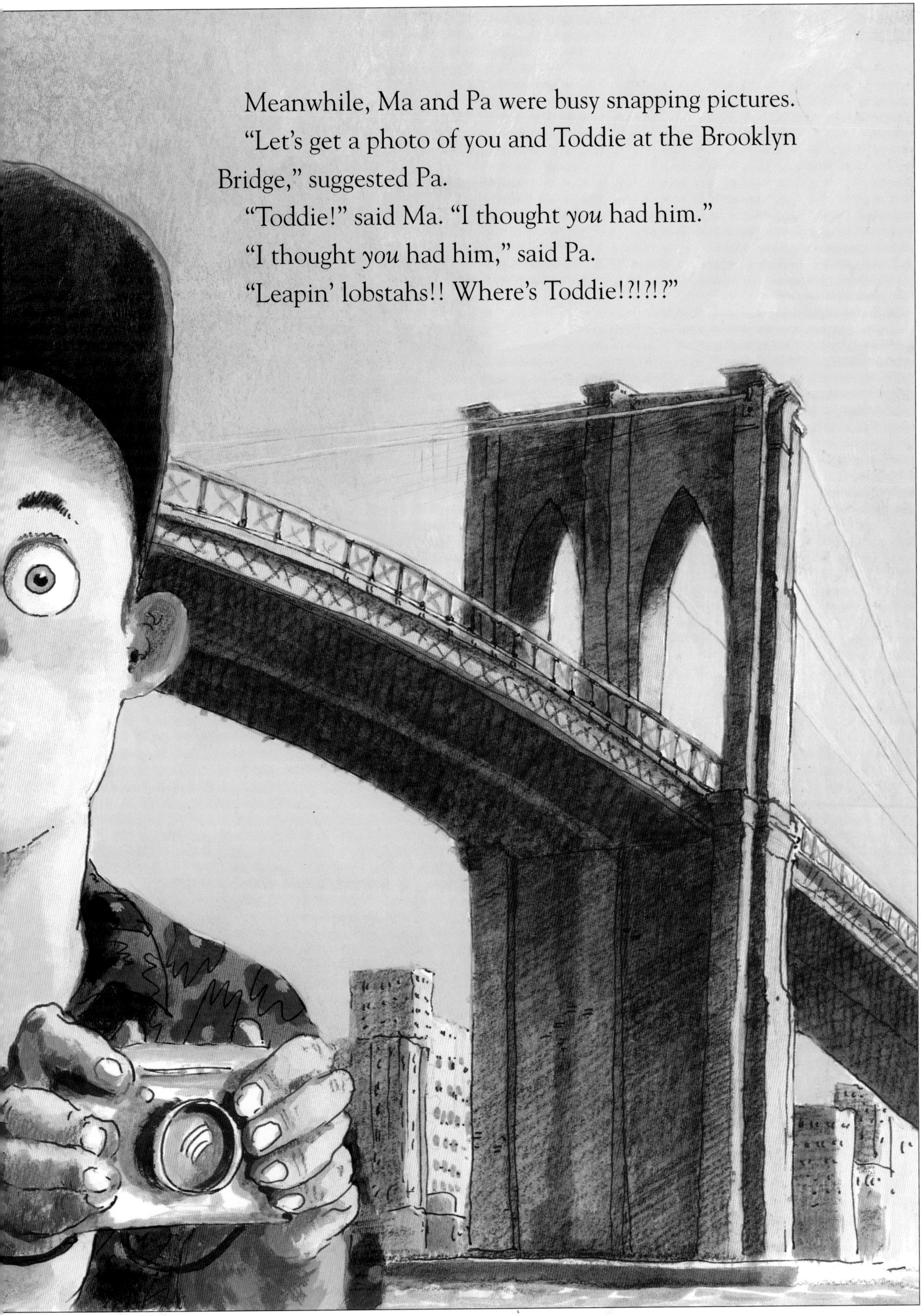

Toddie climbed the tallest building.

"Ma! Pa! WHERE AHYAH?" he called.

He looked all across the city. Then he closed his eyes and listened.

He heard the honk of taxis. He heard the rush of cars, the wail of sirens.

Then he listened harder than he had ever listened before and, far below, he heard two voices.

"Toddie!"

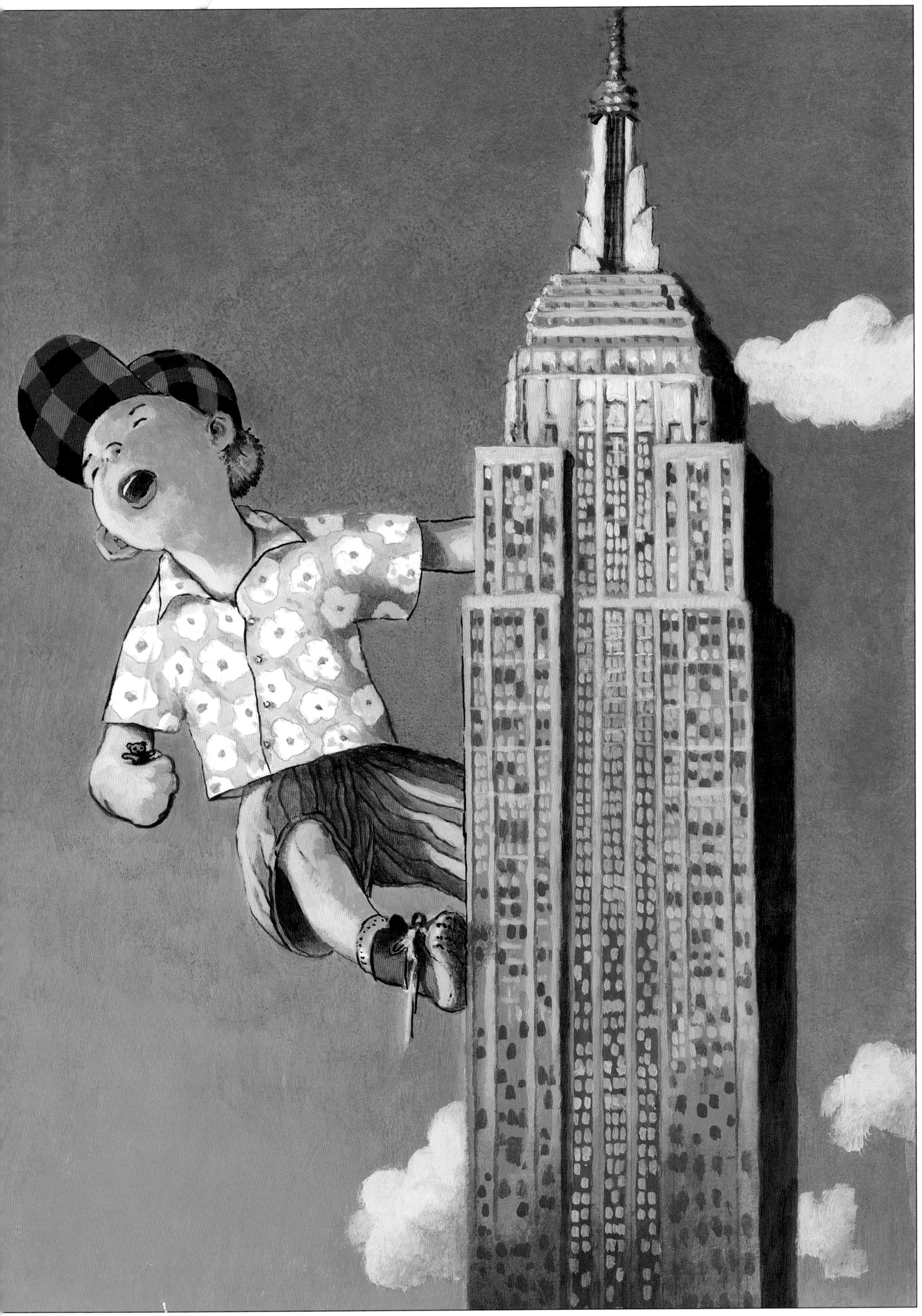

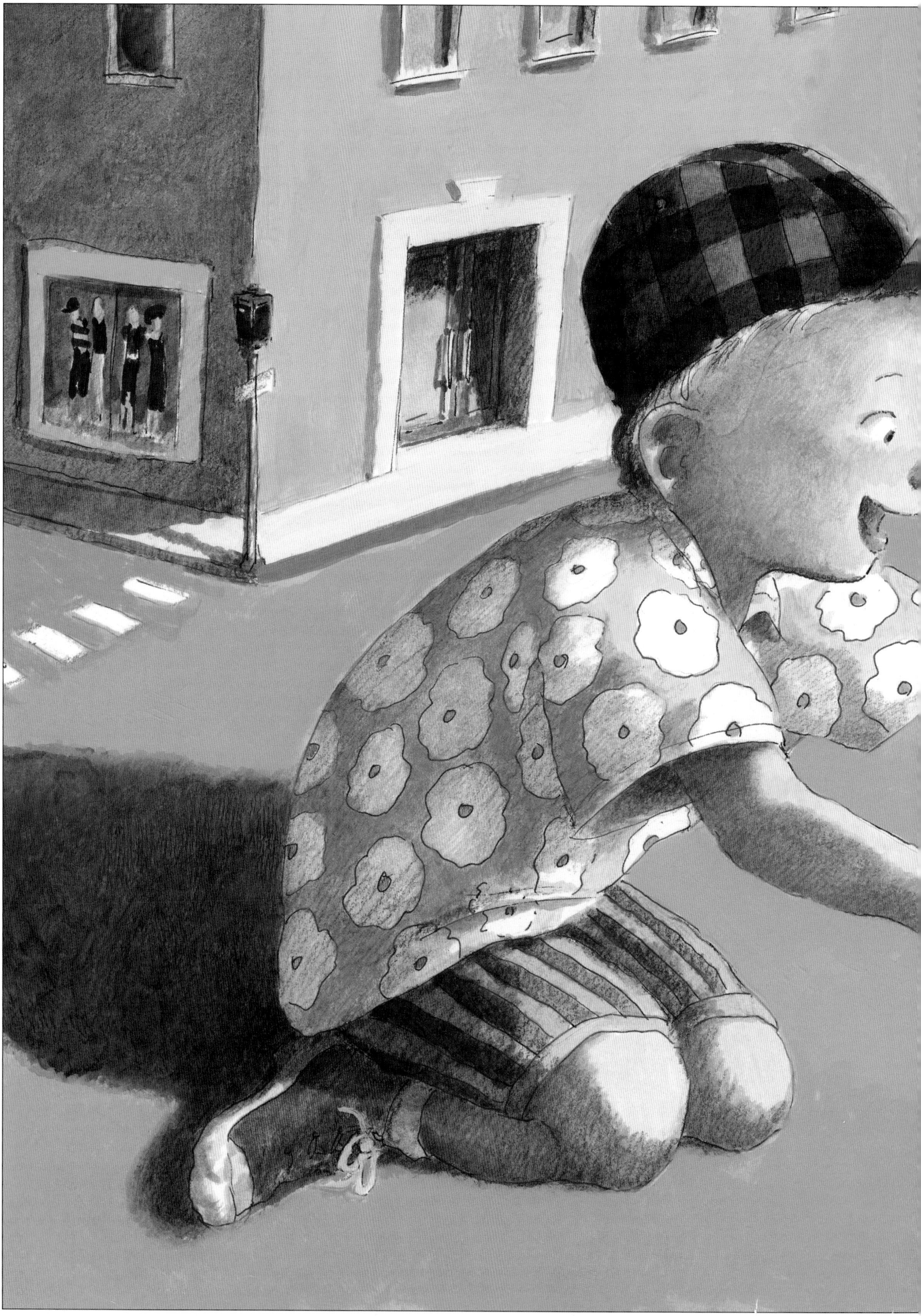

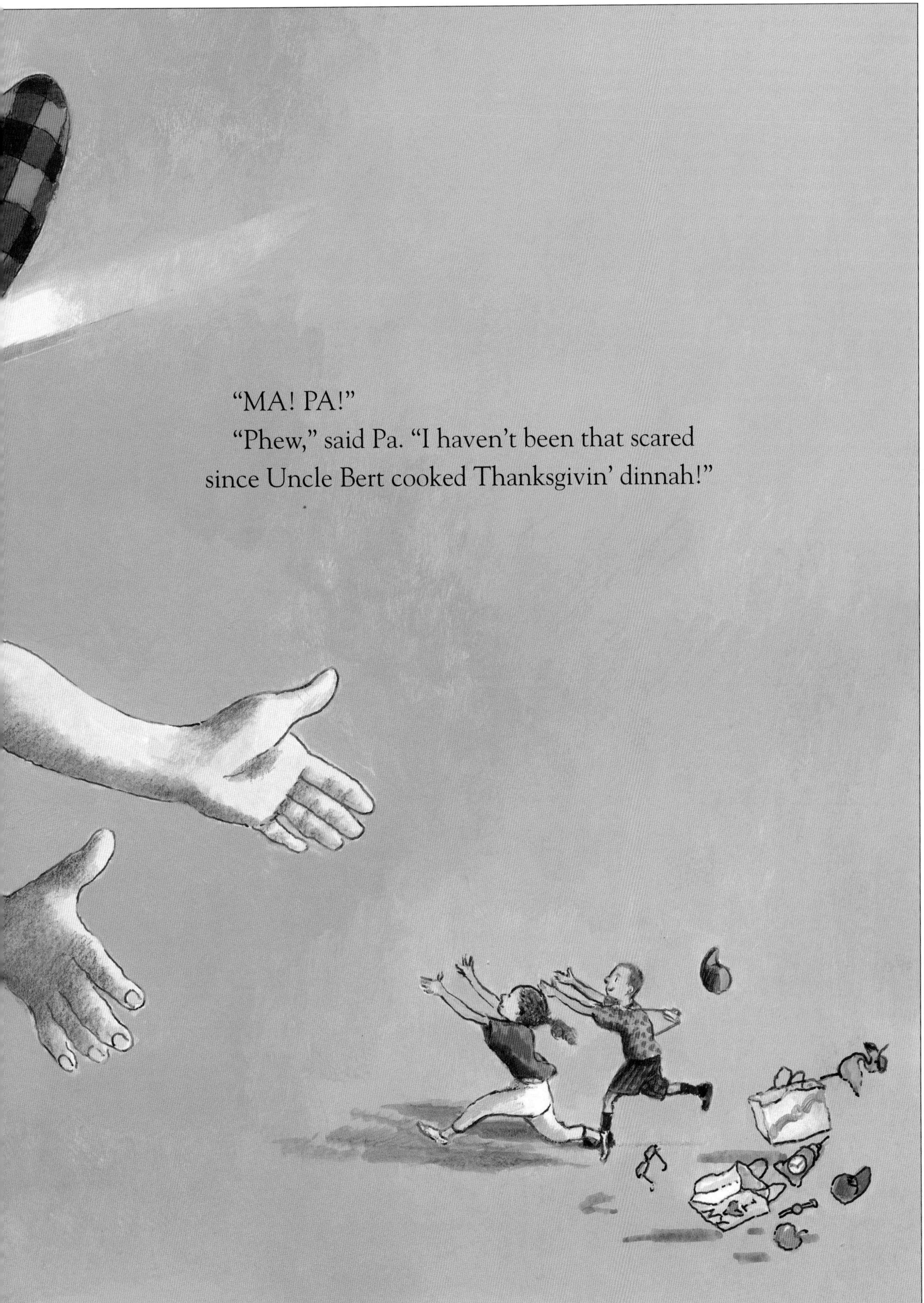

"MA! PA!"

"Phew," said Pa. "I haven't been that scared since Uncle Bert cooked Thanksgivin' dinnah!"

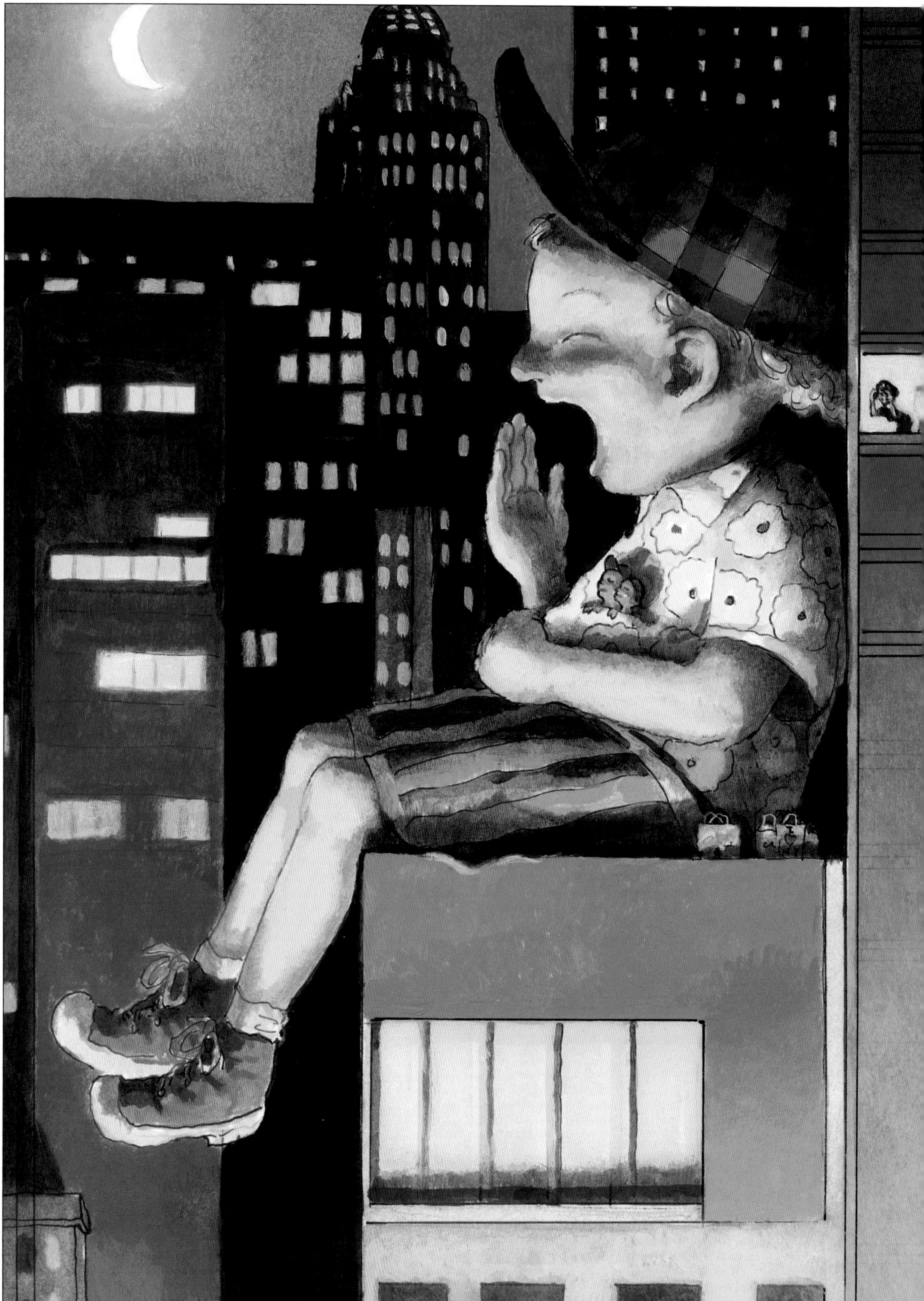

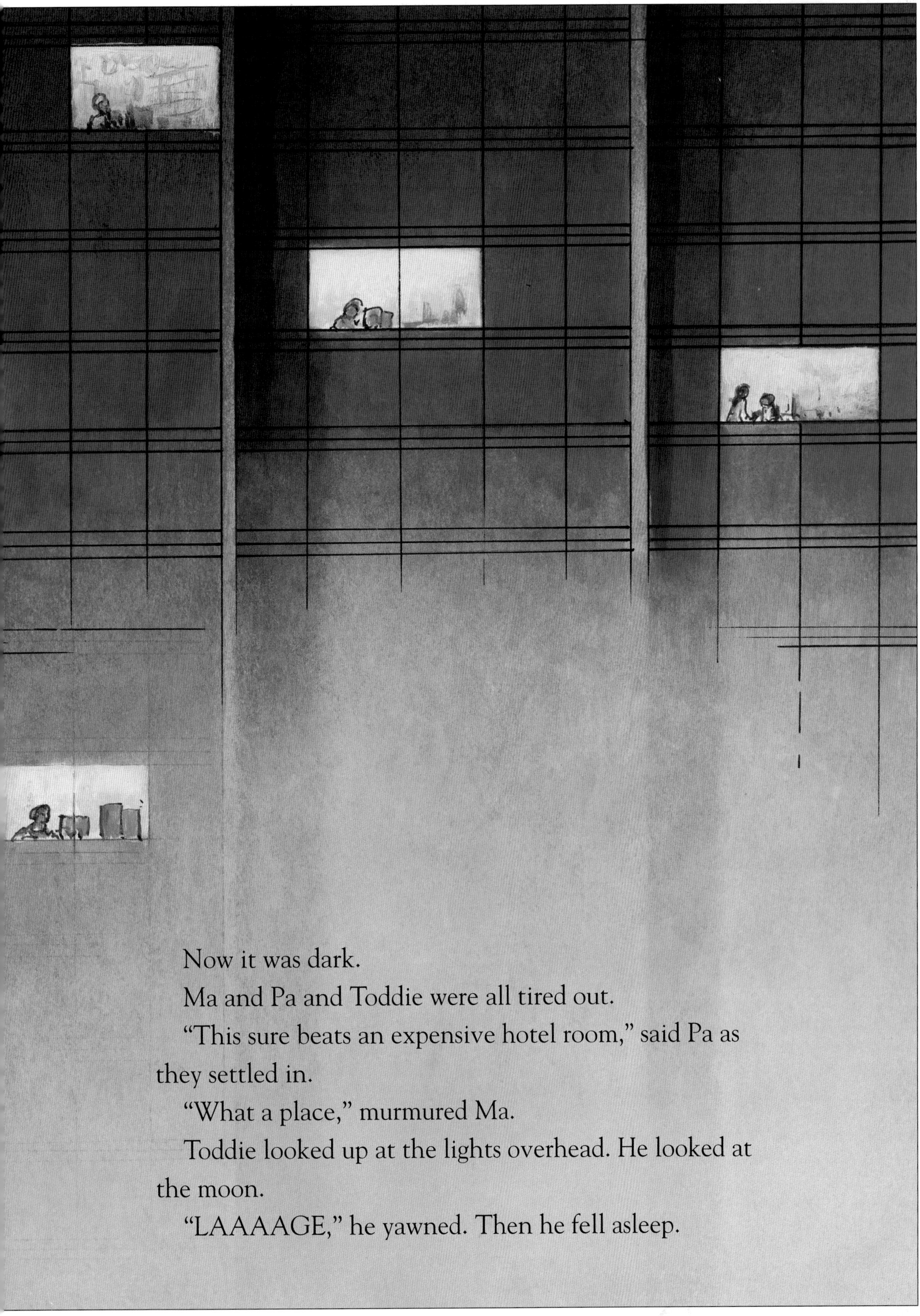

Now it was dark.

Ma and Pa and Toddie were all tired out.

"This sure beats an expensive hotel room," said Pa as they settled in.

"What a place," murmured Ma.

Toddie looked up at the lights overhead. He looked at the moon.

"LAAAAGE," he yawned. Then he fell asleep.

Early the next morning, Ma and Pa said, "We can't leave New York without seeing the Statue of Liberty."

They took the Staten Island Ferry. Everyone on board had something to say to Toddie and Ma and Pa.

"Wicked big ice cream!" Toddie pointed to Lady Liberty's torch. "Home?"

"Yep, let's head home," said Pa.

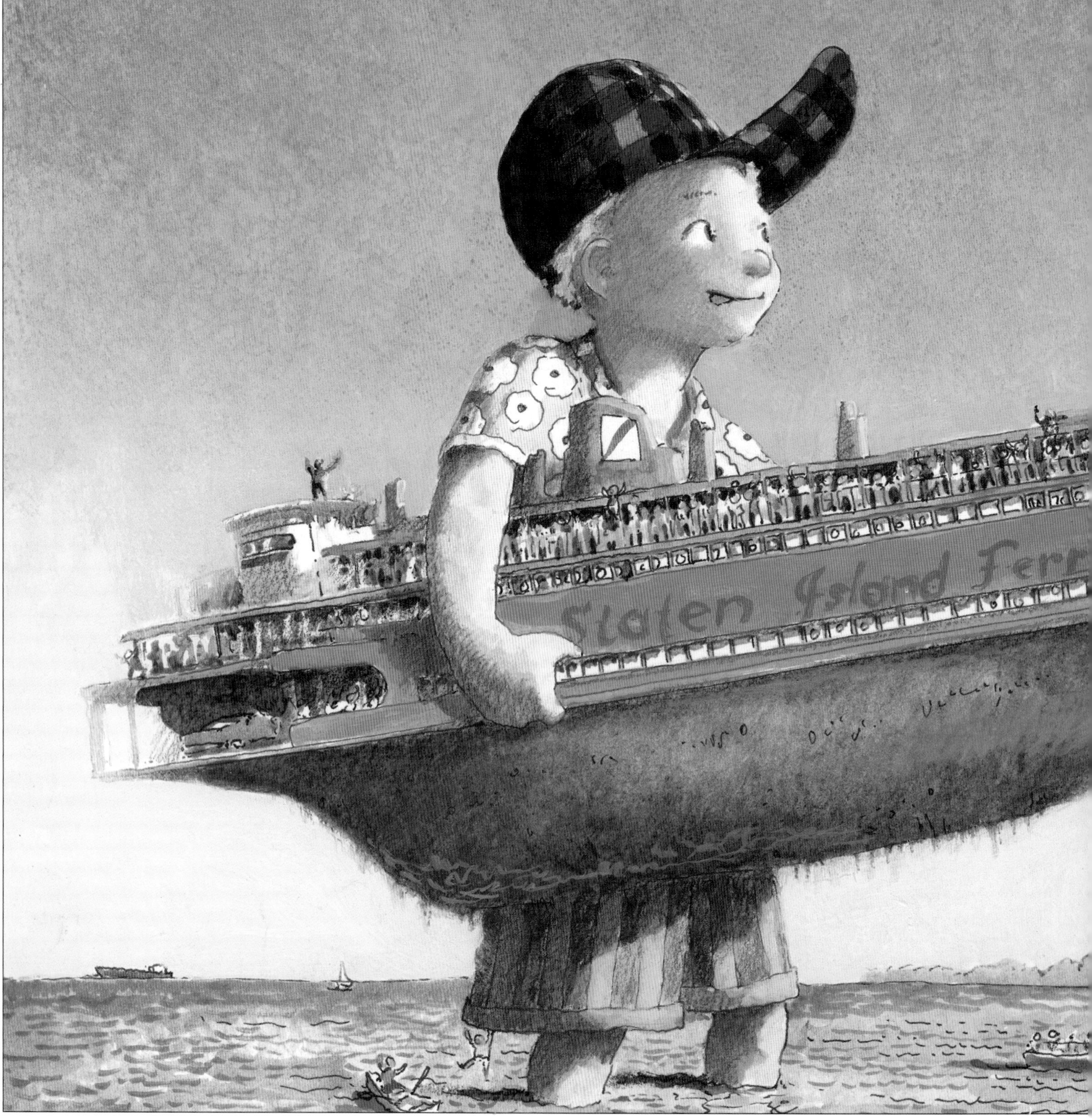
Staten Island

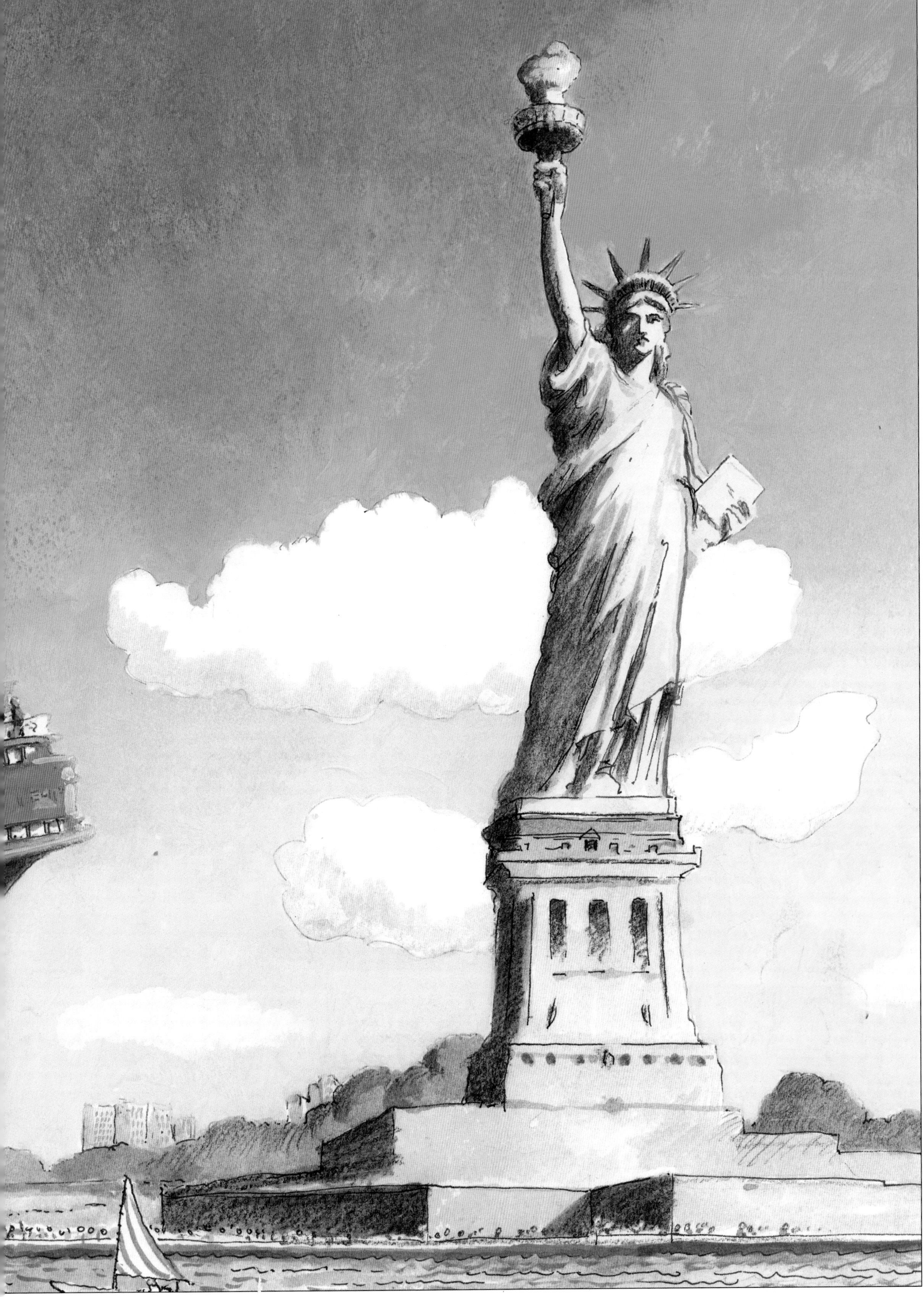

They caught the next train to Maine.

"Ahhhh," said Pa. "There's nothin' like fallin' asleep in your own bed."

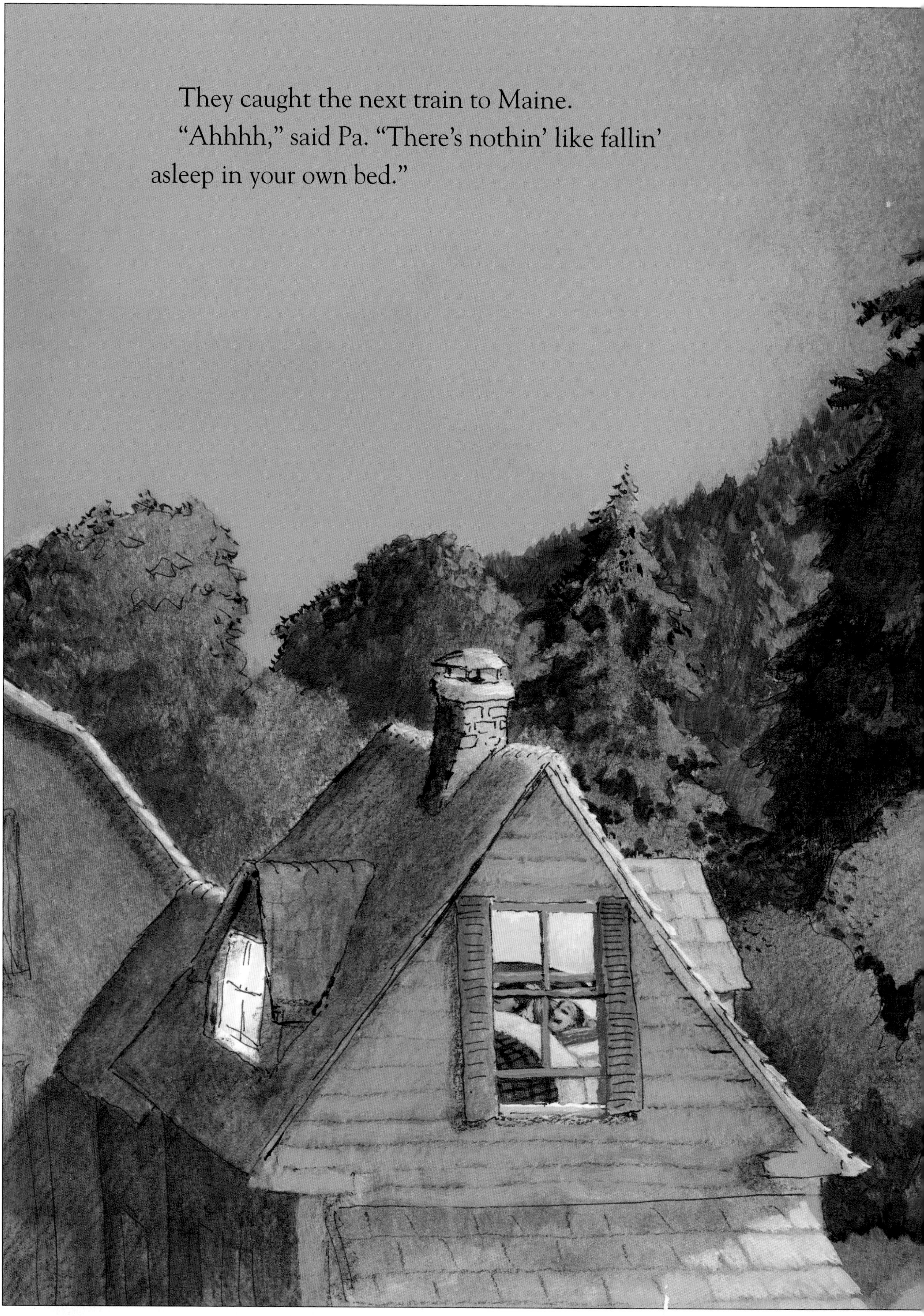

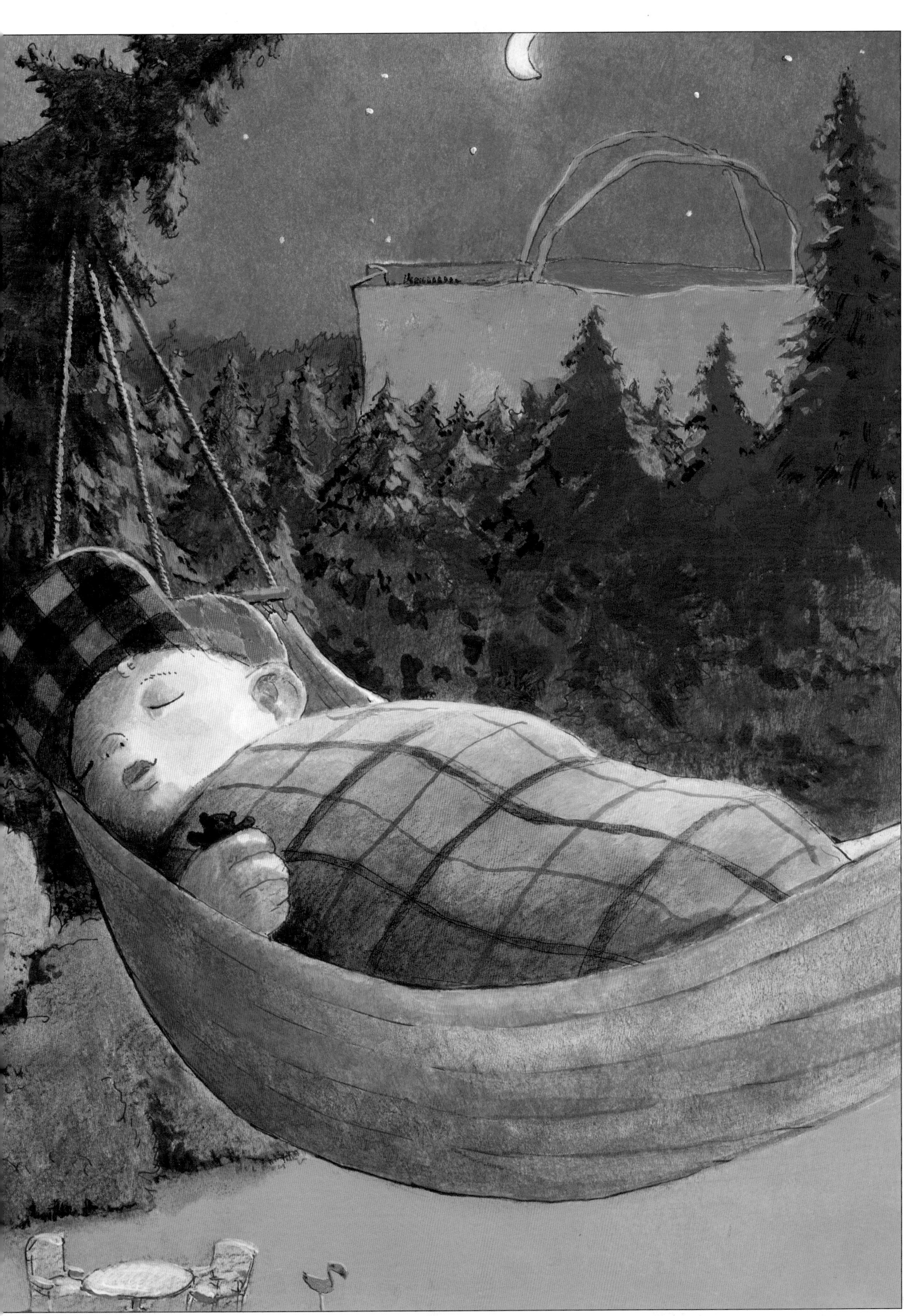

Back at home, Ma and Pa took a look at all of their souvenirs.

"Gosh," said Ma. "It's too bad Toddie never got a chance to pick out somethin' special from New York."

"That's okay," said Pa. "He's just happy bein' in his own backyard."

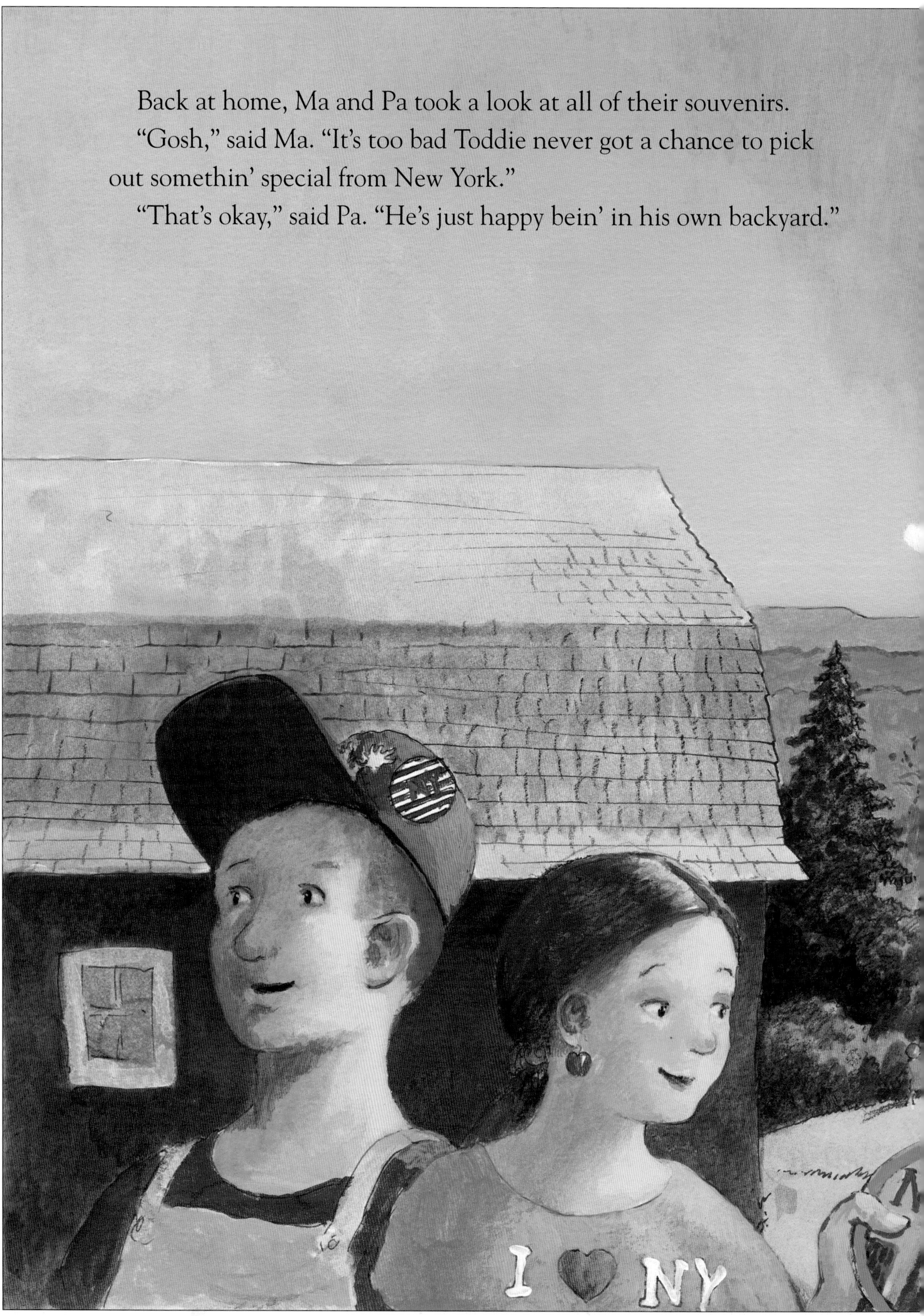

NY
I ♥ NY

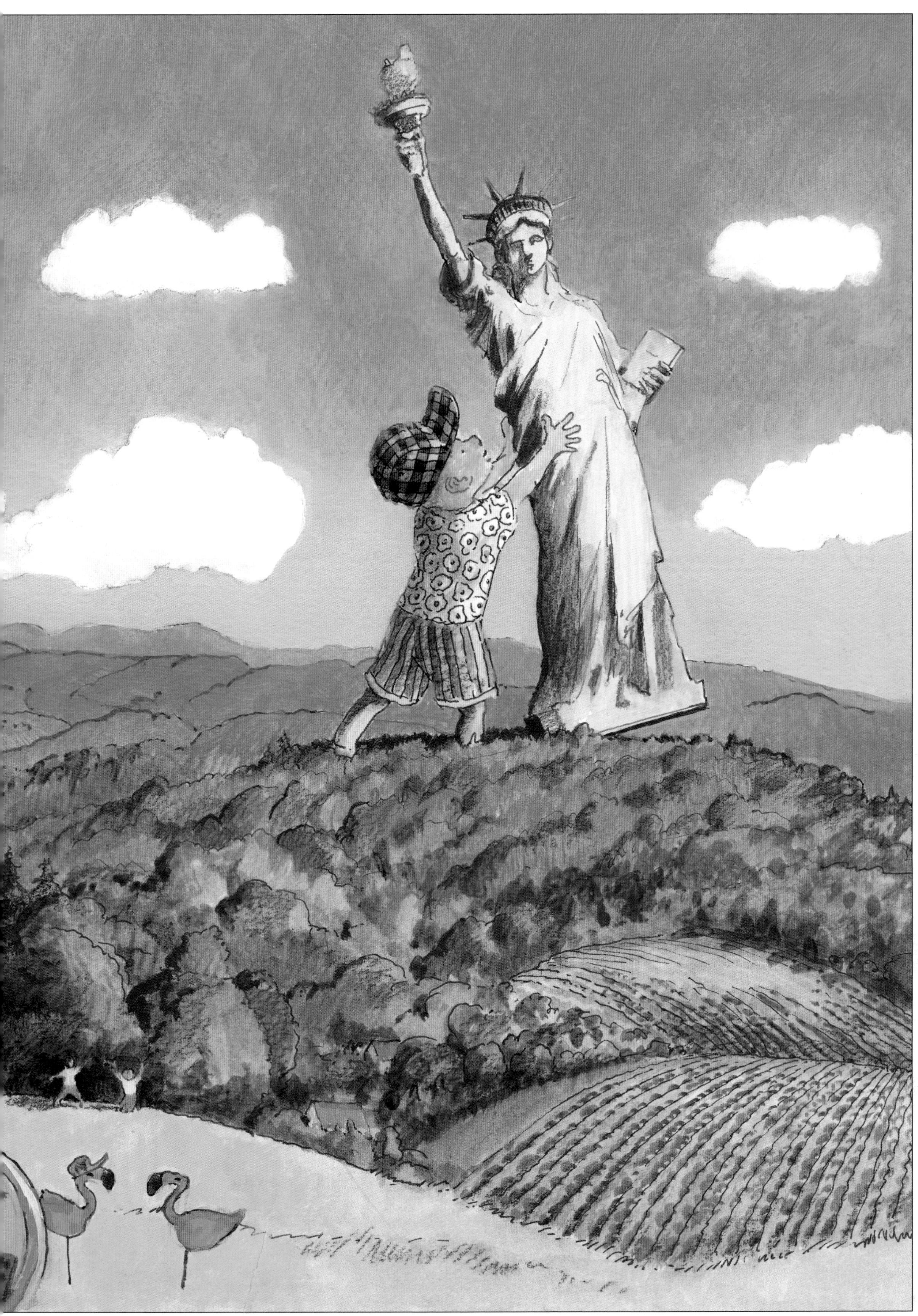

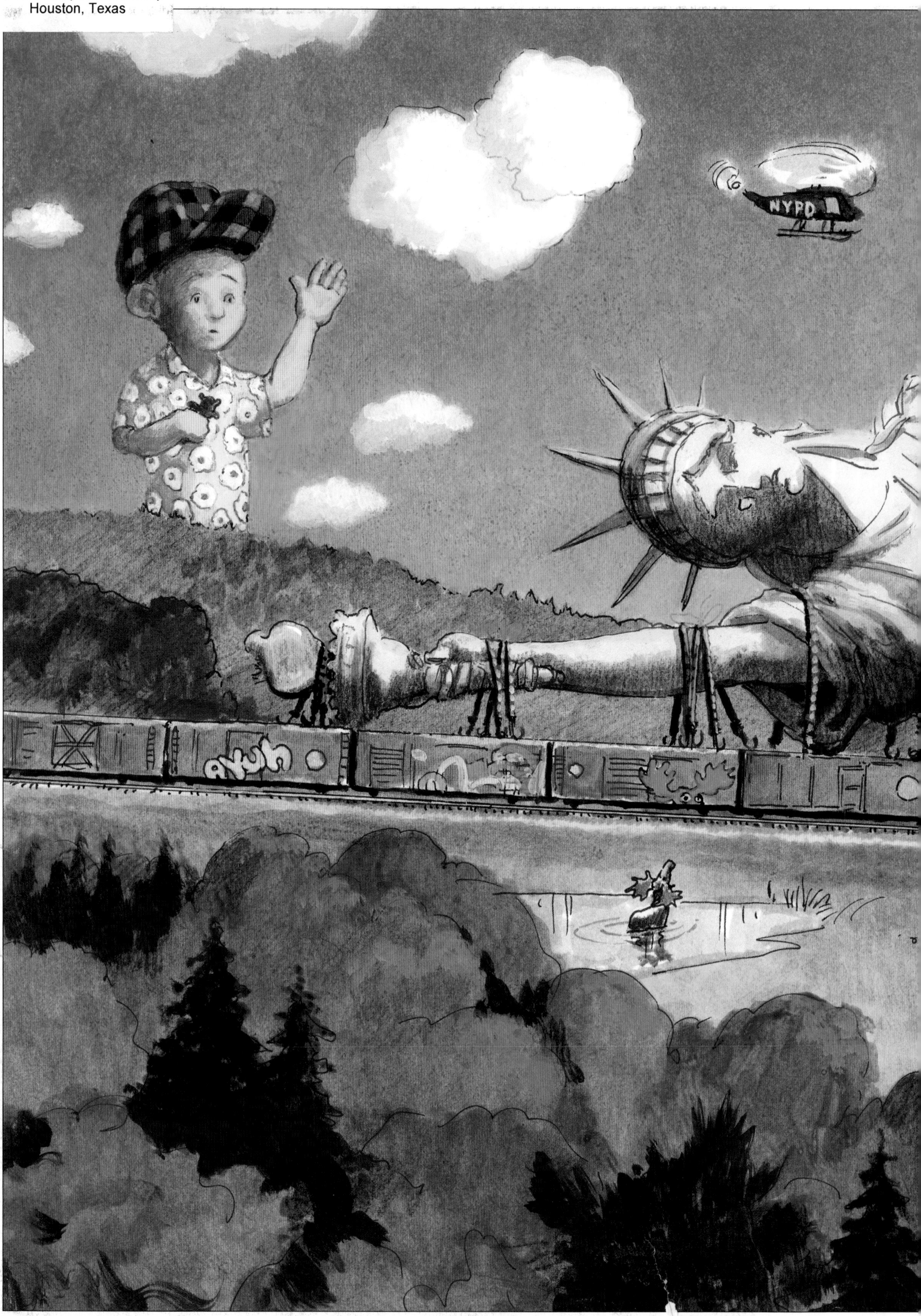
NYPD